Rose From

The Rose Garden 2

Casia Schreyer

An imprint of From the Runes

ROSE FROM THE ASH – THE ROSE GARDEN 2
Copyright ©2017 by Casia Schreyer
E-book edition released 2017
Paperback edition released 2017

Cover © 2017 by Sara Gratton

All rights reserved.
No part of this book may be reproduced, scanned, or distributed in any printed or electronic form without permission. Please do not participate in or encourage the piracy of copyrighted materials.

ISBN 978-1-988853-02-4

This series is dedicated to
The Rooswinkles.

This book is dedicated to my great-aunt, Yvonne Rooswinkle. And to my mother, Yvonne Ediger, who passed away before I had any books published. She was my editor and my Beta reader.

17th of Starrise, 24th Year of the 11th Rebirth
Golden Hall, Capital City of the Province of the Metalkin
Wedding of Mallory Jewel-Rose

Vonica Bright-Rose had never before left the Sun-Temple complex and she was happy for it. She and the three other princesses had grown up there but when they left for their home provinces she stayed behind. The Sun-Temple in the Sun Province would always be her home. She was comfortable there, she was safe there, and most importantly, the people she saw every day didn't stare at her.

The two day long journey north to the Province of the Metalkin was hard for her. She hid in her carriage while on the road and not even her curiosity of the passing villages and farms could make her peer out the windows. Not after the first young man had stared at her and then sneered.

She didn't care one bit if the rooms were small and simple and in some inns barely clean as long as she didn't have to go down to the common room for dinner to be a spectacle for the masses. By the time they reached the high iron gates of the Metalkin Castle in Golden Hall Vonica's lip was raw and two of her fingernails had been chewed short.

Even her curiosity about Mallory Brock, the girl from beyond the Isle of Light and the newly crowned Princesses Jewel-Rose could not draw her out of her guest room more than was required by tradition and courtesy.

At least Rheeya, Taeya and Betha don't stare at me. It is good to see them again. Mary Song, a serving girl who had travelled with them from the Sun Province, finished brushing her hair and started twisting the vibrant red locks up into an intricate pile.

"Couldn't we leave it down?" Vonica asked. She sounded more like a mouse than a princess.

"Tradition, Princess," the girl replied. "It is a royal wedding; you must be properly dressed and adorned."

"Of course."

With her hair done she was ready to go down to the Sun Dome. In addition to the wedding there was also the anointing of the new prince; both were long ceremonies full of tedious prayers, oaths, and incense. Here at least the attention was on the happy couple, though Mallory looked more bewildered than happy, and not on Vonica's scars.

Mallory's prince was certainly worthy of the attention with his broad shoulders clad in a tabard of fine cloth of gold. His hair and thick beard were blacker than wrought iron. When he glanced around the room, his arm around Mallory, his eyes were piercing and dangerous.

A strong man, a strong prince. She's lucky. But of course love comes easily to a woman as beautiful as she is.

Though all five girls had the same red hair, the mark of their covenant with Airon, the chief god, and Vonica's spirit guide, there was no mistaking one for another.

Taeya is a wisp of a girl, Rheeya is solid and feminine, Betha has a round face but sharp eyes and a sharp tongue, thorny her people call her, Mallory is just lovely, and me? These scars make me the easiest to recognize out of all of us.

The priest said the final prayers and Prince Kaelen escorted Princess Mallory out of the temple to cheers and applause from the gathered nobles.

Vonica hardly noticed dinner, or the décor, or the music. She talked with the other princesses but mostly just stared at her plate and tried to ignore everyone who might be staring at her.

They're more interested in Mallory than you, today. On your wedding day they'll all be staring at you.

20th of Starrise 24th Year of the 11th Rebirth
Sun Temple, Sun Temple Province

Princess Vonica was finishing the last of her tea when Mary knocked and let herself in. "Good morning, Princess," she said with a curtsey. "Did you have a good sleep?"

"Yes. It was lovely sleeping in my own bed again." She moved to the dressing table and settled on the low bench.

Mary picked up the brush and started on Vonica's long red hair. "Braided today?"

"I'm tired of braids and twists and pins. You spent an hour on my hair the day of the wedding."

"You looked beautiful."

Her eyes met her reflection's and she clasped her hands tightly on her lap, resisting the urge to touch the uneven skin on her cheek. "Not as beautiful as the bride," she said.

Mary shrugged. "Oh, well, the bride is supposed to be the most beautiful woman in the room."

Supposed to be, Vonica thought. *But what will happen when my wedding day arrives? No amount of curling and braiding and pinning my hair will hide my scar. How could anyone ever consider me the most beautiful woman in any room?*

"I'll just pin it back from your face so it doesn't bother you today. I'll leave the rest loose." She sighed. "I do so love your red hair. Now, it's going to be cool today, the sky is so grey. I'll grab your day dress, the one with the sky blue trim on the collar."

Vonica had to smile. Every morning with Mary was like this with her tasks completed efficiently, accompanied by a near constant stream of friendly, if sometimes one-sided, conversation. She allowed the girl to dress her, only half listening to the chatter. There was a polite rap at the door and Vonica said, "Come in."

Master Salazar Sun-Wise came in and bowed. "Good morning, Princess Vonica. How was your journey to the Golden Hall?"

"Short but it was good to see the other girls again."

"It's good to have you home safe and sound. I'm pleased to see you are up and dressed. Master White-Cloud wants to begin hearing petitions early today."

"I was gone a week, less even!"

"Before you leave for court I had hoped to speak with you."

"Of course. Mary, I'll have my morning tea in the private library after court."

"Of course M'Lady." Mary curtsied, gathered Vonica's laundry, and went out.

Vonica settled at the dressing table again, her attention turned this time to her steward rather than her reflection.

"Princess, as you know, it is critical for the well-being of our province that you find your prince as quickly as possible."

"Yes, I am aware."

"It is my duty as your steward of religious matters to guide you through this process as best I can. Unfortunately the most reliable way we have of finding your prince is to introduce you to each of your suitors one at a time."

"I'm not sure I like the way that sounds. How many suitors do I have to meet?"

"There are thirty suitors among the noble class and another forty or so among the gentry."

"There are seventy men who could be my prince?"

"A little more than seventy, yes."

"Seventy men who all have the same birth day."

"No, Princess. You see we were never sure if the soul left the body immediately at death or if it lingered. And we don't know if it enters the new body at birth or during pregnancy. We have found no set pattern in all the previous generations. There are seventy men who were born within a set time frame following the death of Prince Archibald, the prince of your previous incarnation."

"Will he look like Archibald?"

"We have noticed no pattern or similarities in the physical appearance of the princes, aside from general similarities common to the people of our province."

"So there's no way to narrow that list down?"

"No Princess, I'm afraid not. Master White-Cloud will speak with you further after court today. While you were away he made arrangements with the noble families regarding a schedule for these introductions. If at any time during this process you have questions or concerns you may speak with me."

Master Sun-Wise's knock had been polite and precise, this knock was heavier, more demanding. Salazar sighed slightly and opened the door. Master Antony White-Cloud strode in. "Princess, you have been absent from court for five days. I hope you are available to hear petitions today."

"Yes, Master Anthony. Master Salazar and I were just finishing."

"Of course, Princess," Salazar said with a bow.

"And thank-you for your advice in this matter."

"That is my duty Princess."

Antony waited until Salazar was gone. "Princess, we will be hearing petitions early every day now, with the exception of the day you attend chapel each week. Your lessons will also be shortened during this time. While we were all gladdened by Princess Mallory's appearance, her quick marriage only serves to highlight that you are not yet married. The high-born families are pushing for the honour of introducing their sons to you."

"Please. I'm tired from my trip. Let's go down and deal with the petitions and tomorrow we can discuss my suitors and how and when I will meet them."

"I'm sorry, Princess, but the nobility were adamant. The meetings begin tomorrow immediately after you hear the day's petitions."

Panic threatened to choke her. She reached out and straightened a necklace on her dressing table so she wouldn't have to look at her steward. "At the very least let me hear today's petitions before we discuss this further. Perhaps over my morning tea?"

"Of course, Princess, as you wish. Shall we go?"

Mary had been right, it was cool, and all the sky she could see through the tall, narrow windows in the hall was a dreary grey that threatened rain. It was the season for rain and Vonica knew the farmers would soon be busy in the fields. Still, Vonica preferred to see the sun, she always had.

"My Sunny Girl," Madam Olga had called her when she was very young.

Madam Olga had raised her and the other princesses here in the Sun Temple from the time they were born until Holy Week of their twelfth year.

No, not since birth, since we were brought here, she corrected silently. It had been a shock to learn that there was a whole world outside of the Isle of Light, connected only by a passage through an infinite darkness, and more shocking to learn that she had been born there, not here. *Are my parents alive? Did they look for me? Do they think I'm dead? Oh, I wish I were going to see Madam Olga, she would know what to say about all this.*

Master White-Cloud didn't approve of her spending time with Madam Olga anymore but Vonica still went to visit the older woman for tea from time to time. It was comforting and Vonica knew Olga enjoyed the visits too.

Sunny Girl, Vonica thought. *No one has called me that in a long time.*

She had been nine when everything had changed and she stopped being a sunny, smiling, mischievous, little girl.

They arrived at the hall and the herald bowed to her. "I will go out and announce your arrival to the petitioners, My Princess."

"Thank-you." She saw him smile as he went out. When she heard his proclamation she took her place on the grand chair at the top of the dais. It was made of a pale wood, inlaid with gold and polished until it caught sun and glowed, a beacon of light, a symbol of Airon's presence.

"How many petitioners are waiting this morning?"

"Not many. There are a few who spoke to me while you were away whom I told to return when you had. The rest, I suppose, will be more of the usual."

"I'm ready to begin."

The first petitioner was a finely dressed man who entered with a younger man in tow. Their footsteps echoed in the empty hall and as they walked the light from the tall, narrow windows flashed on the distinct golden ring he wore. It was tradition for court to be open to the public, especially to the nobles who were visiting the temple, and when Vonica had begun hearing cases and petitions Master White-Cloud had insisted she follow that tradition. She'd had fits of anxiety and hadn't been able to sit through a full morning of court until they had removed the audience. All of those people staring at her, it was too much. Just at the thought she felt her heart beat quicken. She took a deep breath and tried to smile. Master White-Cloud would scold her if she didn't smile.

The two men reached the steps and bowed.

Relatives, she decided. *Most likely father and son.*

The father, who introduced himself as Master Sky-Borne, kept his face down-turned as he addressed her. The son openly studied her. She tried to ignore him and focus on the father's petition.

"Have you spoken to the guild about your request?" Vonica asked.

"I have, Princess, and the guild denied me the men I requested. They do not see or understand the need. But if you requested the job be done sooner, if we had a royal request to give weight to ours, they would listen."

"I will speak to the guild before I make a ruling. If at all possible I will help you get the men you need, but if the guild's reasons for denying your request have serious merit I will have to side with them."

"Of course Princess, thank-you Princess."

"Master White-Cloud please send a letter to the appropriate guild master and summoning him to court tomorrow so I can deal with this matter promptly."

Antony nodded and made a note on a parchment he kept at hand.

"Many thanks," Master Sky-Borne said again and bowed. Then he nudged his son. The younger man bowed as well and their hurried footsteps echoed on the marble floor once more.

Antony's assessment had been correct; the list of petitioners was relatively short and as usual was heavily weighted towards the upper class. Vonica was princess over the smallest of the five provinces, both in size and in population; they also had the highest rate of education and the amount of intermarriage between the common born and the lower branches of the noble families made true class distinction difficult. There were, of course, farmers from both Evergrowth and the Animal People living in the Sun Temple

Province, as well as low born smiths, potters, woodsmen, and healers, but they did not seem as dependent upon Vonica to settle their every dispute.

Today the disputes seemed more trivial than usual and the majority of the petitioners had their sons with them. When she mentioned this to Antony between petitions he shrugged and said, "Young men learn business, etiquette, and protocol from watching their fathers."

It is not their fathers they are watching, she thought, relieved to see that the next petitioner was dressed in leathers, a sign he was most likely from the Animal People. Perhaps even more convincing an argument for his heritage was that he did not have a gawking son trailing behind him.

Hearing the petitions of the common and low born took less time than hearing out the nobility and soon Vonica was free from her perch. As she left the hall she told a passing servant, "Please fetch Mary and tell her that court is finished for the day. And remind her to bring an extra place setting for Master White-Cloud."

The servant bowed low and disappeared in the direction of the kitchen.

When they were settled in the study and tea had been poured Vonica said, "What exactly did you have in mind for these meetings?"

Antony set his cup on the table without taking a sip. His eyes were wide and bright and he leaned forward as he spoke. "You will meet each suitor privately and share a meal with them. This will give you time to talk to each of them and get to know them a little. Hopefully one will catch your fancy sooner rather than later."

His enthusiasm was not contagious. "You're sure there are no other ways? I won't know what to talk to them about. Surely this is not the way the other princesses did it."

"In the past there was no need," Antony said. "Your predecessors hosted a large number of their peers here at the Sun

Temple. They attended class together and held dances. Court was open to the public and they often hosted visiting noble families for casual dinners or for tea. You have resisted every attempt anyone has made to befriend you since the other princesses left for their own provinces when you were twelve."

Sadly this wasn't an exaggeration on his part. Vonica had preferred the company of books to the company of people ever since the accident. The other princesses were the only ones she'd ever been close to. After they had left for good her stewards had invited some of the noble girls to stay at the Sun Temple but she hadn't gotten along well with them at all. More often than not she fled in tears to the sanctuary of her rooms or the library.

"I'm sorry," she said, staring down at her tea.

"And you know how difficult it was for you to hold court in the beginning."

All those people watching me, staring at my scars until I couldn't breathe without them judging me.

"We solved that problem by removing the audience. I went against every noble family when I did that."

"You serve me, not them," Vonica said.

"I'm your steward of political matters, My Princess. I serve you by helping you navigate the demands and desires of the nobles. We must keep the peace with them or they will make your rule very difficult and unpleasant."

"Of course," she murmured but she couldn't help but think of how unpleasant it had been having everyone staring at her and whispering about her. Antony denied the whispering when she mentioned it to him but she knew. "Master Salazar mentioned seventy suitors."

"It may be closer to eighty," Antony said.

She took a deep shuddering breath. "Okay, eighty. How did you decide on the meeting schedule? I assume the schedule has already been prepared."

"Yes. It was a complicated matter of selecting those men who were born on the most likely dates and balancing that with the political standings of the families." He preened a little.

"Shouldn't birth date be the only deciding factor?"

"Perhaps if it were a more reliable method of determining the identity of your prince. As it stands the more important families would be insulted if they were not given the chance to introduce their sons first."

"If he's not qualified to be my prince why should I have to meet him at all?"

"It was a concession made during the reign of the second princess, the first rebirth, a hold over to the time before the pact when social standing was the most important factor in choosing spouses, especially for the prince or princess."

"Why are you so concerned with these outdated whims of the nobles?"

"I told you Princess, it's my job, especially since you seem to have forgotten your lessons on political decorum."

"I haven't forgotten," she said. She could feel her cheeks heating up. "I understand completely that the noble families must be treated with respect, but surely the more unreasonable customs …"

"I've done what negotiating I can," he insisted.

"How much time am I expected to spend with each of them?"

"An hour should be sufficient," he said and sipped at his tea.

"An hour?" She set her cup down with a little too much force. Luckily nothing spilled.

"For a first meeting, yes."

"First meeting?!"

"Of course. Every princess said they had to speak to their prince on at least two separate occasions before they realized they were drawn to them. You are the eleventh rebirth which means we have seen this ten times."

"But you can't tell me anything about the process of finding my prince."

"No. Not really. Only that it has always been a unique and subjective experience. All we can note are some patterns."

She sighed. "Fine. We will try this your way, for now."

"Thank-you Princess."

"Will anything else be expected of me today?"

"No, Princess, aside from your usual lessons this afternoon of course."

"I won't miss my lessons. Until then I wish to be left alone." She finished her tea. "Unless there is something else to discuss?"

"Nothing at this time, no. Enjoy your morning."

22nd of Starrise 24th Year of the 11th Rebirth
Sun Temple, Sun Temple Province

Antony paced the small study, his hands behind his back. His white robe billowed around his ankles at every about-face. The midday sun shone in through the balcony catching the cloth of silver threads woven into the green sash that was Antony's badge of office. Every few laps he would pause to look at the ornate hourglass set up on the mantle.

Finally Salazar said, "The hour is almost up, are you really going to pace through the whole thing? Neither the princess nor her first suitor has come barging in here complaining. I'm sure everything is fine." Salazar was seated at the desk taking notes from a large tome.

"She doesn't want to do this," Antony said.

"Many princesses met their princes by chance. It's not often these formal meetings are required."

"Most princesses are more social. They visit with the children of the noble families. They have the chance to meet more people naturally. Our princess is a hermit."

"She's not that bad," Salazar insisted. "You'll see. You may realize that these meetings do more to soothe the egos of the nobility than to find a prince."

They were interrupted by a knock at the door. Both men looked at the hourglass. The last grains of sand were falling.

Antony rushed across the room and pulled the heavy door open. Princess Vonica stood in the hallway. Antony bowed and made room in the doorway for her. "My lady, forgive me for keeping you waiting at the door. How was lunch?" He led her to a chair.

"He's not my prince," she said.

"Now Princess, we won't be sure until ..."

Salazar cut in. He had turned from his work to face them. "I'm not surprised. He was given the privilege of being your first suitor because the last prince was from his family. A silly tradition."

Antony glared at Salazar for a moment and then said, "I'm glad you completed your meeting. I told you it wouldn't be so bad."

"Of course. May I go?"

"Yes, of course you may," Salazar said gently. He was smiling at her, a kindness in his eyes.

"Your history teacher is expecting you for your lessons," Antony added. "And you have a second meeting at dinner tonight."

"No, no lessons today. I think I need to lie down for a while." She pushed herself from the chair and ghosted out of the room.

25th of Starrise 24th Year of the 11th Rebirth
Sun Temple, Sun Temple Province

Though High Priest Balder Sun-Spark lived at the Sun Temple he only officiated over feast days. His main responsibility was to guide the entire island in matters of religious importance and for that he had to spend much of his time in prayer, meditation, and study. Daily services in the main chapel were led by the other priests living in the capital, or on rare occasions, an acolyte. After the Hymn to the Sun and the prayers of thanksgiving to each of the spirit guides he would offer a short teaching.

Vonica went once each week. She sat alone on a bench at the very front of the chapel and ignored everyone else sitting behind her. Now, with the meetings taking up most of her days, this time alone in the chapel was even more precious.

After the service Vonica had the whole day to herself. She spent the morning in her private garden but around midday the rain started. Mary brought her a steaming bowl of soup and fresh buns for lunch. She didn't relish the idea of running into her stewards and being forced to answer more questions about her suitors, all of whom she had so far found wholly unacceptable, so she made her way down to the main library.

The Grand Temple was the heart of the complex, a great round dome-roofed building around which everything else was built. There was the palace, dorms for the priests and scholars, a sprawling garden, and an extensive stable. Vonica's favourite place was the Scholar's Library. There was a private library in the palace wing and the half dozen studies each had numerous bookshelves, but it didn't compare to an entire building dedicated to books. That one building held every book ever written on the Isle of Light in the last fourteen generations, at least.

Vonica loved to lose herself among the shelves, brushing her fingers over the spines of the many volumes. Around her the students, scholars, and librarians worked at the tables or searched for volumes among the shelves. The only sounds were the rustle of paper, soft footsteps, and hushed voices. Here among the pages were the history and myths of all five provinces, stories from times past and far off towns. In the deep corners of the library where dusty books sat mostly forgotten Vonica could pretend she was completely alone.

She was in one of those dimly lit alcoves when she noticed a flickering light between the books. Curious she moved around the shelf on silent feet.

A young man sat at the table, his back to her. He wore a robe and a scholar's brown sash. There were books open on the table before him and a bottle of ink at his elbow. Vonica could hear the scratching of his pen on the parchment. She took another step forward, curious. His hair was long, longer than was currently fashionable among the noble men, and pulled back away from his face. She paused when she noted that the top of her shadow was dangerously close to his shoulder. Another step and it would fall across his work, alerting him to her presence.

She stepped back, slow and careful. Her elbow bumped the book shelf and sent a book tumbling to the floor with a heavy thud. She turned and bolted before he could spin around in his seat.

When he did look all he saw was a fleeting shadow.

Vonica slowed as she reached the central area of the library where the great chandelier hung over dozens of tables. She paused to slow her racing heart and an assistant librarian approached her.

"Princess, a servant was just here looking for you. Your stewards want to speak with you."

"What time is it?"

"The bell just rang announcing dinner in the students' mess, My Lady."

"How long ago were they looking?"

"Not long."

"Thank-you."

He bowed and backed away.

Salazar had convinced Antony to sit in one of the high-backed chairs in front of the fire place but the skinnier man was not sitting still. He'd lean back, then forward, his elbows on his knees, then back again. He crossed and uncrossed his legs. He tapped his feet on the floor. He drummed his fingers on the arm of the chair.

"I don't know why you're so agitated," Salazar said as he flipped the page in the book he was reading.

"I don't know how you can sit there so calmly. This is important."

"We haven't been waiting long. It is her personal day after all, she's allowed to hide."

"But if it's true, imagine! After only six meetings. We could have the wedding in a few weeks."

"Don't get carried away, Antony."

"And Giovanni Great-Spark is from a very prestigious family."

"I'm afraid Airon doesn't care much about the prestige of the noble houses when he chooses the princes for his princesses."

"You really think Airon chooses? I always believed it was a matter of being born at the right time."

"Most people do," Salazar agreed. "I'm not the first steward to feel otherwise. How else would you explain the fact that there is no discernable pattern to the birth date of the princes?"

"I'll leave that matter to the priests."

"Well such matters interest me a great deal."

"Where is she? It shouldn't take them that long to find her."

"The Sun Temple is larger than any other castle on the island. She's not restricted to the palace wing after all."

Antony hmphed and they resumed waiting in silence.

A brief knock had Salazar looking up and Antony on his feet. A servant opened the door and said, "Princess Vonica has arrived."

"Send her in," Antony said. He smiled. "Princess Vonica, I'm glad someone was able to locate you. We have something important to discuss."

"Of course," she said. She followed Antony's gesture and settled in the seat he had just vacated. "What is the matter?"

"One of your suitors came to us today."

Salazar saw Vonica's face go white. "Are you all right Princess?"

She nodded.

"Do you recall Giovanni Great-Spark?" Antony said.

"Supper yesterday," she said. "I promise I stayed the full hour."

"He came because he believes he is your prince."

Vonica was so pale Salazar could see each and every freckle on her face. He closed his book. "Master Great-Spark believes it and Master White-Cloud believes it but I would like to know what you think."

"He's not my prince."

"Princess Vonica, in most rebirths it was the prince who recognized the soul bond first," Antony said, repeating the line Vonica had heard time and again.

"He's not my prince. If you'll excuse me, I don't feel well. I'm going to lie down for a while." She rose from her chair and left.

"She's impossible," Antony spluttered. "How will she ever find her prince if she's not open to the possibility? 'He's not my prince. He's not my prince.' That's all she ever says about these meetings."

"We are not privy to what happened in those meetings, Antony. We have to trust her."

"If she had her way she'd never get married."

26th of Starrise 24th Year of the 11th Rebirth
Sun Temple, Sun Temple Province

Master White-Cloud knocked on Vonica's door. A moment later Mary peered out at him. "Yes M'Lord?"

"I need to speak with the princess."

"She's not here M'Lord."

"When I spoke with her after lunch she said she was coming here to lie down, that she was not feeling well."

"She came here after lunch but then she went on to the chapel. She said she was too restless to lie down."

Antony hmphed and walked away.

The chapel in question was a small room on the other side of Vonica's private gardens. Vonica had only to walk down the flagstone path, past the small, trickling fountain, and she was there. Antony had to walk all the way around since he had not been invited into Vonica's rooms. The hallway took him past his own room, Master Sun-Wise's room, a formal sitting, and a study.

The chapel itself was round with a sun painted on the floor, its points stretched out like the points of a compass. Four small altars were set against the walls at the southwest, northwest, northeast, and southeast points of the sun's rays. These were dedicated, one each, to each of the lesser spirit guides. The main altar to Airon was against the eastern wall. Vonica sat on a low backless bench before the altar, a book open on her lap. Antony could smell incense, something with rose petals in it, as he entered.

"Princess, forgive my intrusion but it is nearly dinner time."

Vonica glanced up. "Of course. I must have lost track of the time. I'm on my way."

Antony nodded once and retreated from the holy sanctuary only to come face-to-face with Salazar. "She's in there?"

"Yes. She's on her way. I'll see to it that dinner is prepared and laid out in time."

Salazar went into the chapel. "Princess, I just wanted to check that you are feeling okay."

"Why wouldn't I be okay?"

Salazar frowned. Whenever they spoke to the princess about her suitors her voice took on this hollow quality, and he was hearing it again now. "I know you are not overly fond of people."

Vonica's smile was a sad one. "That's where you are wrong," she said. "Don't worry about me. I know my duty and I will do it."

"Then I will leave you to prepare."

The last grains of sand trickled down to the bottom half of the hour glass silently announcing the end of the hour. Salazar and Antony held their breath, waiting for a knock at the study door. The seconds stretched into minutes.

"What do you think?" Antony said.

"I think she made it through the hour or we would have heard something sooner."

"Do you think they're still talking? Do you think he's the one?"

"No," Salazar said but Antony was already hurrying for the door.

He found the door to the small dining room open and servants clearing the food from the table. The princess and her suitor were both gone. Antony turned on his heel and marched to the princess's room. A moment after he knocked Mary opened the door a crack.

"Is she here?"

"She is M'Lord but she's changing. You'll have to wait."

He stayed in the hallway outside her door, his arms crossed and his foot tapping. Finally the door opened and Mary stepped back to admit him saying, "Princess, Master White-Cloud is here to see you."

"Thank-you Mary."

"I'll be back in a moment with your tea." Mary bowed and left.

Once alone with the princess Antony said, "How did dinner go?"

"He's not my prince."

"I find your resistance to this process most frustrating, I must admit."

"I'm sorry, but he's not my prince. I don't want to meet with him again; it would be a waste of time."

"Princess, I don't believe you are truly giving these young men a fair chance."

"I'm staying for the full hour," she said.

"Fine. Fine. We'll continue tomorrow."

"I don't know. I don't feel well."

"All you need is a good night's sleep and a good breakfast. Good night Princess. I will see you for court tomorrow."

"Please find Mary and tell her I've changed my mind. I don't feel like tea tonight after all."

"Certainly." He left with a bow.

Vonica hung her robe and crawled into bed, pulling the downy-stuffed blanket over her head. In the darkness she was finally free to cry.

27th of Starrise 24th Year of the 11th Rebirth
Sun Temple, Sun Temple Province

Court was over for the day and Vonica had changed from her working dress to something fancier as dictated by Master White-Cloud. *I'm not going to start wearing ball gowns every day just because I get married. Shouldn't he see me as I really am?* Her fingers went to the scar. *No one sees me as I really am. All they see is the scar. Or money. Or a fancy dress. Or political power.*

She took a deep breath, put on a smile, and went into the dining room. Her suitor was already there, they were always early for these meetings it seemed, and he rose as she entered.

"Princess Vonica, I am Mannix Light-Flame." He bowed. "I am honoured by this chance to meet you."

He was smiling and it was actually a kind smile, and he was looking into her eyes. Some of the tightness in Vonica's chest eased. "Welcome. Please, have a seat and we shall begin the meal."

Servants appeared, setting dishes of food on the table. As each passed her she said a soft, "Thank-you."

Mannix Light-Flame said nothing.

When they were alone he said, "I must say, they have done a beautiful job with the gardens this year. It's early spring and already everything is so green."

"You are interested in gardens?"

"Only far enough to appreciate a beautiful one. I tried to grow a little garden in my window when I was young. The gardener at our keep said I over watered them for a week straight before neglecting them completely. I'm afraid a young mind is easily distracted and of course I haven't any real talent for making things grow."

"It must be lovely to be able to make things grow," Vonica said wistfully. "Where is you keep?"

"Not far from here. We're able to come to the temple for all the major feast days."

"How fortunate."

"I've seen you before you know. I always looked for you on feast days. All the kids did. When all the princesses lived here we made a game of guessing who was who."

Vonica remembered getting up to all sorts of mischief with her friends when they still lived here at the temple with her so she could easily imagine a group of children, bored at a High Feast service, indulging in all sorts of games, and it made her smile.

"Of course the game changed as you grew older and they started dressing each of you according to your province." He was studying her. "The boys would sit and tell stories about your scars."

Her smile was gone. "My scars?"

"Of course. We all wondered how it happened. There were always whispers about it but no one seemed to know for sure. The adults always shushed us. Even now, no one speaks of it openly. My sister stayed here awhile to be one of your companions after the other princesses moved away. She said you were rude and stuck up and never spent any time with them. Even she doesn't really know what happened, and she tells me she once asked."

The whole time he had been speaking Vonica's face had gotten paler and paler making the scar stand out even more. "I don't want to talk about it," she said in a hushed voice.

"Don't you think your prince and future husband has a right to know?"

"You are not my prince," she said. She pushed away from the table. "Excuse me. I don't feel well all of a sudden. I need to lie down. Excuse me."

As she fled the room she could hear him shouting, "Our hour isn't up yet. You can't leave!"

She didn't look back. She hurried down the halls but didn't run; running would attract too much attention from the servants and guards. She couldn't go back to her room; her stewards would find her there. Mannix would go to them and complain and they would drag her back and lock her in a room with him for a full hour no matter what she said.

The library. I can hide among the shelves and the shadows. The books ask no questions.

She nodded as she passed servants and scholars but she didn't slow down. *Any moment they could be behind me. They won't listen to me!*

She slipped behind and between shelves until she was deep in the ancient records section. She slowed and leaned against the nearest shelf, only now realizing tears were trickling down her cheeks. She wiped them away roughly with the pack of her hand and took a deep shuddering breath. It smelled of dust and parchment and dry leather. She took another deep breath, calmer this time.

Nearby she heard something tap against glass, a faint sound. She moved to the end of the shelf and spotted the flickering glow of a candle behind the next shelf. She eased forward.

As far as she could tell it was the same young man at the table as she had encountered two days earlier. He was hunched over his work. She could hear the scratching of his quill on the parchment, punctuated by the tapping of the tip against the ink bottle. Somewhere further off someone coughed. Inside she sighed. She longed to stay here, to watch him work, but she had to find a place to hide.

Unwilling to take her eyes from him until she had to, Vonica took a step backward, her hand on the shelf to prevent another bump. And she caught her heel on the hem of her dress. She caught herself on the shelf but a tiny "oh" of surprised escaped her lips.

He turned in his chair. She wanted desperately to turn and run, even if it made her look like a scared rabbit, but his stare pinned her in place. After a long, heart-pounding moment he said, "Were you looking for a book in this section? You can borrow one of my candles."

"No," she stammered. "I'm not."

"Oh. Would you care to join me then?"

"I don't want to interrupt you."

"You're not."

"What are you studying?"

"Oh, I'm not a student." He got up and went around the table, away from her. He pulled out the second chair. "Please, join me."

There were many bottles of ink on the table. The candles glinted red off one and green off the next as she moved past them. "You're an artist," she said, pausing.

"I'm illuminating a manuscript for Master Agoston Bright-Quill."

She relaxed. A true artist would look at her and judge her, just like her suitors did. Illuminators just filled in the decorations on a manuscript and while it required talent and an eye towards detail it was mostly copying the style of others and the subjects were portrayed in simplified form. She took the offered seat.

"Thank-you. I've met Master Bright-Quill before. He is very passionate about his work."

"You're being polite, aren't you?"

She blushed.

"You can be honest, I won't tell him."

"He's blustery," she said. "And over confident."

"More honest but still polite. I'm sure your stewards would be proud of your diplomacy. He's pushy and pompous. His brother is a lord in another province, his cousin is a guild master in the Capital, and he claims there is a prince in his direct ancestry. A great-great uncle I believe."

"There was Archibald and before that Maximus, and before that Joffrey."

"That was it, yes. Joffrey Bright-Quill."

"There are so few twice-named families in our province that in a few more rebirths every family should be able to boast that honour."

"The greatest honour becomes the greatest equalizer. Until a family is chosen twice."

"What are you working on?"

"Master Bright-Quill's collection of legends concerning Prophet Abner."

"He brought all the provinces under the guidance of Airon, didn't he?"

"That's right."

"Is it interesting?"

"The subject matter is but sadly Master Bright-Quill's pompous attitude comes through in his writing. I thought you would have learned about Prophet Abner in your studies."

"I did, but it was a brief lesson that focused on dates and unity and balance. And it was many years ago."

"These legends are some of my favourites which is why I requested to work on this project."

She leaned forward resting her elbows on the table and her chin in her hands. "Would you tell me one of the stories while you work?"

"Of course."

"Princess? Princess Vonica?" The voice was still distant but it made her sit up.

"I'm sorry. They're looking for me."

"Will they look here?"

"I don't know. I should go." She pushed away from the table. "Thank-you."

"If you come back I'll tell you that story."

"All right. I'll come back in five days. After service."

"I'll be right here."

She started to leave but paused at the book shelf. "I didn't get your name."

"Johann."

"Good-bye, Johann, I'll see you in a few days."

"Good-bye My Lady."

28th of Starrise 24th Year of the 11th Rebirth
Sun Temple, Sun Temple Province

She'd gotten lucky. She missed everyone who was looking for her and made it to her room undetected where she crawled into bed more out of boredom than anything else. She woke to twilight shadow and a dinner tray on her desk. She ate, read a little, and went back to bed.

Her luck ran out as soon as she was out of bed. There was a knock on the door and she assumed it was Mary come with her breakfast and to help her dress for the day so she said, "Come in."

It was not Mary but her stewards. She pulled her robe closed.

"Ah, Princess, you are awake. I hope you are feeling better," Salazar said.

"Better?" She blinked at them, confused.

"Yes," Salazar replied. "We found you asleep before dinner and assumed you were not well."

"Of course. Yes. I am feeling better. I just needed the extra sleep."

Salazar nodded. "We made apologies to your evening suitor. He will see you today."

"Thank-you."

"Your disappearing act has put you two meetings behind schedule," Antony said. The words burst out of him.

More confusion and she turned from Salazar to Antony. "Two? I only missed one meeting yesterday."

"You did not complete your meeting with Mannix Light-Flame yesterday so you will meet him again today."

"No."

"Yes."

"Please. Master Antony, please, I can't. He's not my prince. Speaking to him, listening to him, it soured my stomach. Please don't …"

"That is enough," Antony said. "It is inappropriate to speak of a guest in this manner. You will do him the common and expected courtesy of a full hour of your time."

There was no way out so Vonica switched tracks. "Fine. But I will require a guard in the room for the entire hour."

Master Anthony's eyes widened and his mouth dropped open. Behind him Master Salazar smiled.

"You can't be serious," Antony said.

Bolstered by that smile Vonica stood a little straighter. "I can and I am."

"My Lady, to post a guard *in* the room, to imply a suitor cannot be trusted …"

"I am implying no such thing," Vonica replied.

"But surely having a guard in the room would hinder your conversations. I mean, prevent you, or your suitor, from speaking your mind."

"That's the point."

"Princess?"

"Master White-Cloud I have nothing further to say to Master Light-Flame and quite frankly I am tired of listening to what he has to say when he is 'speaking his mind'. I will be polite and the guard's presence will ensure that Master Light-Flame is also polite. You wouldn't want him to become verbally belligerent, now would you?"

"Of course not," Salazar cut in. "We will see that it is taken care of."

"The Light-Flame family will not like this," Antony said.

"Then lie. Tell them that the guard is there to supervise me, to ensure that I remain in the room for the entire hour. If that doesn't appease them, too bad. Now, if you will excuse me I must prepare for court."

"Of course Princess," Salazar said with a bow. He stared at his companion until he too bowed. "We shall see you shortly. I am glad you're feeling better."

When they had gone Vonica's knees began to tremble and she sat down on the edge of the bed before she fell. Standing up to them like that always took so much out of her which is why she didn't do it often.

When Mary came in she said, "M'Lady, are you all right? You look so pale. Shall I fetch the healer?"

"No, thank-you. I'm fine."

"Are you certain? You slept so much yesterday and now I can see every freckle on your face from here."

"I'm fine. What did you bring for breakfast this morning?"

"Simple, M'Lady, on account that we didn't know who you were feeling. I can fetch more if you'd like."

"I don't even know what there is yet," Vonica said, smiling.

"Oh, of course. I'm sorry. There's warm bread with preserves and tea and fresh apples."

"That's plenty," Vonica said. "I'll want something simple for court this morning and something plain for my hair."

"Of course Princess."

32nd of Starrise 24th Year of the 11th Rebirth
Sun Temple, Sun Temple Province

Vonica sat through the morning service in sullen silence. She tried to clear her thoughts and open her mind to the priest's teachings but it was no use; all she could think of was the damned meetings. She'd attended four of her required six meetings these last few days. She knew the two that had been pushed back had complained. She had a feeling that even the four she had spent time with had complained about her short answers and persistent silences. Antony had visited her daily to remind her to be polite and keep an open mind. The only way to avoid him was to crawl into bed and feign sleep or hide in her private chapel pretending to pray.

Well he can't bother me today no matter how much he would like to schedule extra meetings. Today I spend in the library with Johann, if he has not forgotten.

As soon as the service finished she went to the library, her steps hurried by the fear of running into her stewards, or, worse, a suitor trying to steal a few minutes of her time. They weren't permitted in her wing of the palace but here in the library everyone was welcome.

She found Johann working at the same table and joined him with a smile. "Good morning."

"Good morning, Princess. You look well this morning." Already his inks and books were spread across the table.

"Well enough I suppose. I'm anxious for all this to be over."

"You mean the suitors?"

"Of course you would know about that. I'm sure everyone in the entire Temple Complex is discussing it at length."

"It's important to them."

She sat up straighter, her body and voice becoming stiff. "Yes, yes, I know. I have a duty to my people. I need a prince to bring them all peace and security."

"I'm sorry, I get the feeling that wasn't the answer you were looking for. How many more meetings do you have?"

"Too many. I've barely started and I'm already tired of every one of them staring at my scar. It makes me not want to go anymore."

"Your prince is waiting for you to recognize him," Johann said. He was staring at her but his eyes were firmly on hers and full of soft emotion, not cold curiosity.

She lowered her gaze. "I know. I don't want to disappoint anyone, but …" Her hand went to her cheek and tears sprang up in her eyes.

"Is it so bad?"

"I'm ugly."

"Your prince doesn't think so."

"You don't know that," she said, her fear making her voice bitter and hard. "No one knows that. I'm the first princess in the history of the rebirths to bear such a scar."

"I'm sorry. I didn't mean to upset you."

"No, I'm the one who should be sorry, I'm just feeling annoyed. It's not your fault. Let's talk about something else. It's my day of rest."

"I'm afraid my job is not a very interesting point of discussion."

"You mentioned a story last time I was here."

"I thought you were being polite and indulging me. History doesn't interest most people, just dusty scholars like me.

"Are you as boring as my history instructor?"

Johann chuckled. "I can certainly try to be."

She made a face.

"What do you want me to tell you a story about?"

"Oh, tell me a story that takes place far away from here. I never get to have any adventures of my own."

"Master Bright-Quill found a story about Prophet Abner and King Gregor of the Stone Clan. Now, this is a period of legend and no one at the time wrote anything about Abner, nothing that survived anyway, but Master Bright-Quill's studies led him to different images and themes that were too repetitive to be coincidence. The Prophet was tasked with the near impossible task of convincing the other people that Airon was the chief spirit guide and that Airon had in fact sent him on this errand. Fool's errand, everyone called it. Priests of the spirit guides from across the lands rejected him and many threatened him. Who would ever believe the spirits of their ancestors to be weak or less?"

"But they did accept Airon; we know they did, at some point, because that's how things are now."

"Exactly, but how? King Gregor called for Prophet Abner and gave him a challenge. If he could win the challenge then Gregor would bring all his people into unity with Airon, but if he lost he would agree never to teach against the spirits of stone and earth ever again."

"What was the challenge?"

He set his quill down. Her wide eyes and the story's narrative demanded his full attention. "King Gregor took Abner to a mine, deep inside, down many tunnels and around many corners, until they were far below the mountain. He blew out the lantern and there in the dark he said, 'Here is the power of my people. Here is out deepest mine. There is no way the power of Airon can reach us here.' But the

Prophet called on Airon and there in the deepest mine beneath the tallest mountain there appeared a great light, as bright as the sun."

"That's not possible."

"It's a legend, Princess."

"That's really what the legends say?"

"There is some variance to which king it was, if it was Gregor or his father or his father's father, and which mine the story refers to. There's one version where the king even locks Abner away in a dungeon cell beneath the castle with no windows and no candles. But they all say the same thing; Abner called on Airon and Airon brought the light of the sun there in the deepest reaches of the earth where the spirits of stone and earth are strongest."

"And that was it? The king was true to his word?"

"Well, the legend said the king had the room double and triple checked for tricks but his priests and engineers found nothing that could have created the blinding light. After that he agreed that Abner had passed the challenge and pledged himself and his people to Airon."

Vonica sighed. "I've been downstairs in the archives and that was dusty and dim but to be under a mountain. How dark and close that must be."

"You seem happier now," Johann said. "You're smiling."

"I am, thank-you. I'm sure I distracted you from your work though."

"I did get something done. You know. I'm here every day."

"You have work to do and I have meetings."

"Come between your meetings. I will tell you stories and cheer you up. I know lots of good stories, and even a few poems. And maybe you can tell me stories of the other princesses. It's not likely I'll ever get to meet them."

"I'd like that."

"Then you'll come?"

"I will try. I do have duties that are expected of me."

"Of course. Your job is far more important than mine."

"With all your stories why aren't you writing books?"

"That's a long story best left for another day I think."

She laughed. "Are you trying to bribe me with stories?"

"Of course not. Not at all. Well, maybe a little. But only if I can get away with it. Is it working?"

"I'll see you soon Johann."

"I hope so My Lady."

When he was certain she was gone he packed up his ink and the manuscript into the leather satchel he carried. It was an impossible idea but he had to ask anyways. All he could do was hope that the right people would be willing to hear him out. And believe him.

36th of Starrise 24th Year of the 11th Rebirth
Sun Temple, Sun Temple Province

Firsts, lasts, and centers were considered most holy in all things. That meant that after Holy Week, the five day celebration of Airon and the other spirit guides, the first, eighteenth, and thirty-sixth of each month were considered special. Priests believed signs and portents were more likely on these days and blessings given were more powerful. They were favourable days for weddings and namings.

For Vonica this last day of Starrise held nothing special, just more scoldings. For nearly an hour before her first meeting she sat in the study while Antony White-Cloud ranted about her failure of duty and her deplorable manners. She sat mostly silent, answering only when he stopped talking and glared at her. Half the time he didn't stop long enough after a question for her to answer at all.

She looked regal, sitting still and straight-backed, her hands prim on her lap. Though Master White-Cloud paced Vonica kept her eyes on the vase on the table. Her silence was nothing more than a mask.

Inside she was not nearly as still. Her heart hammered in her chest; she was surprised no one else heard it. Her stomach was roiling and she wasn't sure her breakfast was going to stay down. She knew she wouldn't be eating at lunch. Her throat was dry. Her thoughts were a chaotic mess. She tried to focus on Master White-Cloud's words but her own inner voice had much to say. One was agreeing with Master Antony and adding a few harsh words of its own.

"Failure" was said often, as was "useless". Another was making soothing sounds and offering reassurances. Yet another kept reminding her to pay attention.

By the time he was finished talking Vonica was certain he'd repeated most of his rant three times over.

"Am I making myself clear?"

"You've made your point, yes," Vonica said as politely as she could muster. "I only wish you would listen to me in return."

"I have been listening. All I hear is your refusal to even consider one of your suitors as possibly being your prince."

"Then you are hearing without truly listening. If you'll excuse me? I would like to have Mary fix my hair before …"

"No."

She paused, half out of the chair. "No?"

"Already this week you have disappeared before or between meetings and not reappeared at the appointed time on more than one occasion. No. Your hair is fine. Your dress is fine. I will wait here with you until it is time for lunch."

She wanted to argue but what could she say? He'd already called her out on her real reason for wanting to slip away from his watchful eye. She settled in the chair again, poised and calm. "As you deem fit."

Silence descended on them. Vonica kept her attention on the vase and focused on keeping her expression blank. Antony never took his eyes off of her. He coughed to clear his throat and shifted in his seat. She made no sound. Even when there was a knock at the door she waited quietly and allowed him to answer it.

"We're ready sir."

"Thank-you. I will bring her."

Vonica followed behind Antony all the way to the private dining room.

"Keep an open mind," he hissed.

"Always," she said.

Her suitor, another Sky-Borne, fancied himself a musician and after eating a very small plate of food he proceeded to play for her. She was expecting him to be awful but she found she actually enjoyed it, at least when he sang hymns and folk songs. The songs he claimed to have written himself were not as good.

After particularly well played songs she applauded and in the pause between pieces she asked him questions. "Who taught you to play?"

"There was a scholar at our estate. We all took lessons. I have a cousin who plays but the others either had no talent, no interest, or both. Neither. Do you play?"

"Not really, no."

"Sing?"

"No. Well, under my breath at service, if I really like the hymns."

"I'd like to hear you sing."

"No, you wouldn't. But you could sing another for me."

So he did.

At the end of the hour she marched into her stewards' study without knocking. "Estevan Sky-Borne should remain on the list. I would like to have a second meeting with him. I will be unavailable until dinner."

She didn't wait for them to protest before marching out again. She made her way to the library to spend a few hours with Johann as she had been doing nearly every day. And today she would try harder not to stay too long.

3rd of Cloudrise 24th Year of the 11th Rebirth
Sun Temple, Sun Temple Province

"Good morning My Lady. How was service this morning?"

Vonica smiled. Usually he sat with his back to the opening between the shelves. Today he was on the other side of the table. "The same as every morning I suppose," she said.

"I didn't realize you went every morning."

"I don't."

Johann glanced up at her. "Huh."

"What are you drawing this morning?"

"An ancestor of yours. Actually, how does that work? The last princess was not your mother, so …"

"Is that common knowledge?" She finished fussing with her skirts and settled in comfortably.

"Among scholars who study the history of the royal line I would assume so, why?"

"When I was a girl my educators were vague on that matter. I knew about the magic and the soul bond and that I am the eleventh princess since the pact was made. It was not until very recently that someone saw fit to explain to us the idea of reincarnation or the fact that I was not born on the Isle of Light at all."

"I had heard rumours of that. So it's true then. Must have been quite the shock."

"Yes, that's putting it mildly. Princess Betha was particularly upset.

"I'm sure hysterics are a perfectly acceptable reaction for a young woman who receives that type of life-altering news."

"Oh, she appeared fairly calm, actually. But her choice of words? Well, she made the guards blush."

"I see." He busied himself with his work.

"So I don't know how you would describe my lineage. I am Vonica, the same Vonica who ruled eleven times before."

"Ten."

She stared at him until he squirmed in his chair.

"If you're the eleventh then only ten ruled before you." He cleared his throat. "Sorry."

"The same Vonica who ruled *ten* times before, or so they tell me. It's the same soul and yet I remember nothing. I never met my predecessor. She had to die in order for me to even be born. I must have parents somewhere. Through the portal, where Mallory is from. Do they know I'm alive? Did they look for me? Did the guards who took me tell anyone over there what was happening?"

"When they told you did they have any answers?"

"No. They hardly told us anything. And after the wedding I was whisked back home so quickly. I never had the chance to ask Mallory questions."

"But you wanted to stay?"

"Oh yes. Rheeya and the other girls left here twelve years ago. I saw them once in that time, and that was for a brief meeting called by High Priest Gold-Spark just days before the party was sent to find the Metalkin Princess. They were not permitted to stay long. And then a wedding so soon after, I was excited to see them again. I'd never been to Golden Hall before. I didn't even get a chance to look at their libraries."

"That's unfortunate. But we have the best library on the Isle of Light right here."

"But I wanted to see the gilded chandeliers and speak with the scholars there."

"Why didn't you stay longer? Surely if the Golden Hall is safe for the Metalkin princess then it would be safe for you."

"Thank-you. That was my reasoning. But no, apparently I am too busy to waste time on such a lengthy visit." She could hear both anger and bitterness in her voice. Usually it was easier to hide it but around Johann she found it difficult to keep her emotional mask in place.

"You could have given an order. You're the princess after all."

"It doesn't work that way. Not anymore. My stewards control me and ever part of my life. It's pointless to argue with them."

"You're the princess. The chosen one of Airon."

"They would be happy just to prop me up in front of people on special occasions. They don't need me."

"They need you to keep the balance."

"To keep the balance and do my duty and get married!"

"Vonica ..."

"Sixteen men and only two who didn't make me want to vomit or hide or step into the hearth and let the fire finish what was started sixteen years ago! And what does it matter anyway? Why do they all stare? An accident and now I'm nothing but a scar."

"Is that what you believe?"

"It's hard to believe otherwise when that's all you hear over and over again. No one asks me if I like music or what I like to read. Always it's 'how did you come by that scar?' until I want to scream."

"What do you like to read?"

She sucked in a breath and held it, and then she burst out laughing. When the laughter subsided she wiped her eyes. "Thank-you. I'm sorry; you didn't need to hear all that."

"I'm serious you know. I would like to know what you enjoy reading."

"Oh – uh – um, anything that doesn't take place here in the City or the Temple Complex."

"Anything?"

"The more adventure the better. I will never have any real excitement of my own."

"Your life will not be boring."

"Ah, yes, I have so many dinner parties to attend and petitions to grant and a single garden to walk through whenever the weather is agreeable. And the royal ball! How could I forget that?"

"What royal ball?"

"The one my stewards are threatening me with."

"I see. I'm not sure if I can help you with a royal ball but go to the shelf there."

She followed the direction he pointed and set a hand on the shelf. "Here?"

"One up. The third book from the edge. Yes, the thick one there. Take it down. You'll enjoy it." He slid one of his candles to her end of the table. "Let me know when you to get to good part."

The book was very old, an explorer's account of a trip across the narrow sea to the Far Banks. As soon as Vonica came across that tidbit of information she looked up. "This was written before the pact!"

"Yes, it was. I believe the first Vonica was born roughly twenty years after that account was brought to the library for safe keeping."

She looked down at the book again, her eyes wide. She ran a finger over the page. "Oh wow," she whispered.

"Old books are the best."

"I didn't know this existed."

"I don't think very many people do anymore. There are a few people I know who would love to read that account. You're the first person I've shown it too."

"Why do you keep it a secret?"

"Maybe I'll tell you someday. Read it and tell me what you think of it."

She studied him for a moment but he had gone back to work and seemed unaware of her scrutiny. She adjusted the candle and looked at him again. Still nothing. Even when he reached for his ink he didn't look at her. Vonica turned her attention back to the book and soon the sea captain's tale had her enthralled.

Johann kept his eyes on his work. He wanted her to read the book, partly because it was interesting and he knew she would greatly enjoy it but mostly it was because it would give him the chance to study her. So he waited, even though he could feel her eyes burning into him. He waited until he heard the flip of a half dozen pages before chancing a glance in her direction. She was totally engrossed.

He could see what all the others saw, the red hair that was the sign of Airon's touch upon her soul, the fine cut clothes, a sign of her royal lineage and wealth, and of course, the scar. It started high on her cheek bone turning the side of her face an angry red-purple. The untouched cheek was smooth, the scarred one was rippled and pock-marked. The scar stretched down her neck and disappeared under the collar of her dress.

It was startling and noticeable, he understood that. He didn't understand people's obsession with it, not hers, not her suitors'. It was a scar. Most people had them. He had one or two himself, the result of having an older brother and lacking any talent with a sword.

He turned his attention to the finer and far more interesting details of her appearance. The upturn on her nose and the way she caught her lip between her teeth when she read something exciting. Between flipping pages her fingers drummed an irregular staccato rhythm on the table, muted though so as not to attract the attention of any students who might have been searching for a book nearby. He liked her like this and smiled.

She must have felt him staring, or perhaps she noticed his pen had fallen silent. Either way she glanced up just as he smiled.

"What?"

"Nothing. Just wondering if you've gotten to the part with the herring yet."

"No. Why?"

"Nothing. No, keep reading. Please."

The look on her face told him she wasn't convinced and he made a point of tapping his pen on the edge of the ink pot as he started back to work.

They spent the rest of the morning in companionable silence. Sometime later a bell chimed in the distance, calling the time. Johann looked up from his work but Vonica was still reading.

"Lunch is ready in the student dining hall."

No response.

"Are you hungry?"

"Mmm."

He wasn't sure if that meant 'yes', 'no', or 'pardon?'. He stood. "They don't usually allow us to bring food in here but I'll see what I can smuggle in."

She flipped the page.

He picked up his leather satchel and paused but she didn't look up. He made his way to the front of the now nearly deserted library. From here he headed into the scholar's complex. Lunch here was always simple but something like soup would be impossible to carry back with him. Luckily today they had a selection of buns stuffed with meat and onion. He took four and slipped them into his back with a quick glance around. He grabbed one more and took a bite as he headed for the door.

"Johann Sun-Song, you've been making yourself scarce lately."

"Errol! What have they got you doing?"

"Teaching. Can you imagine?" Errol Sun-Spear chuckled. "They gave me a small band of boys, all around fourteen or fifteen. Mostly I'm to ensure they have their basic history and arithmetic. They're only interested in chasing young girls at court."

"Were we any different?"

"I certainly wasn't," Errol said, chuckling some more. "But you weren't interested one bit. But where are you now? They've got you holed up in some dusty corner, haven't they? They're wasting your true talent."

"I don't mind. You sometimes find untold treasures amid those long-ignored shelves."

Errol shook his head. "Always with your nose in a book. There's more to life friend."

"Perhaps."

"Impossible, that's what you are. Fine. Go back to your books. But don't be such a stranger."

"I'll try, but Master Bright-Quill keeps me busy."

"No excuse. You should come into the City with us one day."

"Perhaps. It was good to see you again."

"And you."

Johann hurried back to the library, eating his bun quickly. He slipped into the library, nodding to two scholars who were on their way out. He made it back to the table without further interruption. Vonica was still reading. Johann smiled and slipped back into his chair. He pulled the first bun out of the bag, tore it into four pieces and set two of them on a napkin. He slid the offering across the table.

Without looking up Vonica reached out and took the first. He kept putting pieces out and she kept eating them and the whole time his smile grew wider. He withheld the last piece and watched her reach for it. Her fingers hit empty napkin and she felt about for something that wasn't there.

She looked up. "Is that all?"

"I thought you'd never put that book down." He handed her the last piece.

"It's a very good book."

"I know, I've read it." They smiled at each other.

"Did this really happen?"

"There's no reason to believe that it's fiction. We have record of strangers coming here before the pact. In fact, their greed is one of the reasons we placed ourselves under Airon's protection. How far are you?"

"He's just making his second voyage to the Far Banks. I can't believe some of the things he describes."

"Yes I recall his descriptions were vivid."

"But are they accurate?"

"No one can know for certain. Except the new princess. Scholars must be fighting for her time."

"But this was written eight hundred years ago."

"Give or take a hundred years or so, yes."

"Would Mallory know anything about what her world was really like eight hundred years ago?"

"Our world is not so different now than it was before the pact."

"Because of Airon's protection and the balance we maintain between the Guardian Spirits."

"So the priests teach."

"Mallory had never heard of Airon before coming here."

"I forgot you've already met her."

"Yes. At her wedding. Last princess found, first princess married. And here I am, the chosen princess of Airon's people and I've got no hope of finding my prince."

"Tell me about the other princesses."

Vonica looked up, startled. She was used to people placating her or scolding her when she started down the path to self-pity. She considered the question and then said, "I miss them terribly and have ever since they moved away. I wish more than anything that I could visit them. Especially Rheeya."

"Ah. Now that tells me a great deal about you and not so much about the others."

Vonica blushed.

"Why Rheeya?"

"We were very close as children. Taeya was so quiet and Betha was so pushy. Somehow they got along just fine."

"Really? I'd always thought the Evergrowth princess would be quiet and gentle."

"The Thorn of the Evergrowth they call her. While Taeya is called the Dove Princess."

"I have learned something new today."

"Do you have any brothers or sisters?"

"Yes, an older brother and a younger sister."

"I suppose that growing up here with the other princesses was like having sisters. We fought but we got up to some great mischief too."

"Now those are stories I'd love to hear."

"Maybe another day."

"Are you bribing me with a story?"

"Is it working?" She smiled sweetly, opened the book, and resumed reading.

5th of Cloudrise 24th Year of the 11th Rebirth
Sun Temple, Sun Temple Province

After court Master White-Cloud settled in one of the arm chairs in Vonica's rom while Mary did her hair. When she was ready he escorted her to her first meeting. The room was empty. Before she could ask Antony about this lack of a suitor when a young man stumbled in behind them. "I'm late, I'm sorry, I was …" He stopped and fixed his clothes, a linen robe and the brown sash of the scholars. Then he bowed. His golden hair fell in his face and he pushed it back as he straightened.

"Princess Vonica, it is an honour to be introduced to you. I am Adorjan Hearth-Glow."

"A pleasure to meet you."

Antony bowed. "I'll leave you two to lunch. I'll see you in an hour."

"I know another Hearth-Glow," Vonica said as they sat.

"That is possible. I have older brothers and cousins and many female cousins and a few sisters. I'm the only eligible suitor in my family though."

"Hmm … maybe that's it. I'm sure I know that name. Oh, of course. There's a Master Hearth-Glow in the employ of Princess Rheeya."

"Yes, my uncle, Alessandro Hearth-Glow. I aspire to follow in his footsteps as a master scholar and steward."

Even if he had changed from his scholar's robes into clothes befitting a noble-born she still would have known him for a scholar.

As he reached past her for the biscuits she noted the ink on his fingers and the cuff of his robe. She smiled. *Just like Johann in that way.*

"Unfortunately I am too young to be a royal steward now and too old to be selected as a future steward for any of the princesses."

"Too old? But you're only twenty-four."

"Exactly. Your current stewards were trained when they were in their early twenties and your predecessor was in her fifties. The lucky men who will replace the royal stewards are only infants now."

"That's too bad."

"It really is. Still, many lords in the province keep a steward on staff. I can hopefully find work with one of them."

"Why do you want to be a steward?"

"I love books. I love to read. That's why I was late, or nearly. I got caught up with a book this morning. But I am afraid of being trapped here with the other scholars. I want to use my knowledge. I want to meet people."

"Have you considered teaching?"

"Oh yes, but my teachers say I am not cut out for it. Oh damn." He knocked the jam over and it oozed, sticky and bright red, over the table cloth. "I'm sorry. Pardon my language. And my clumsiness." He was trying to scoop the jam back into the little jar. Instead he bumped the two pronged fork on the meat platter. It clattered, making him cringe. "Sorry."

She smiled. "It's no problem." She rang a little bell and a servant came in. "Please clean this up," she said.

The servant nodded and a moment later the jam was righted, the worst of the spill was gone, and they were alone again. Adorjan's face was flushed.

"I'm truly sorry. My sisters and cousins are all truly graceful and I'm just clumsy."

She was still smiling at him.

He took another deep breath and returned the smile.

"You know, this has been the easiest meeting I've had to sit through so far," she said.

"You're not falling in love with me, are you?"

The look of genuine and absolute terror on his face startled her and she stammered, "No, I was thanking you."

He turned an even brighter shade of red, right to the tips of his ears. "Oh. Sorry. So, uh – um …" He reached for his tea and she was surprised he didn't spill it.

"Uh, so why don't you want me to be in love with you?"

"It's not like that. I mean, you're the princess, anyone would be lucky to be your prince. I just feel called in another direction. I came here to fulfill my family's duty to the crown. I think you're wonderful but I'm not in love with you. Is that awful?"

"No. It's refreshing. I wish all my suitors were this honest with me. Tell me, Adorjan, what were you studying this morning?"

"Oh, I was reviewing trade treaties between the provinces. It's a tricky business, with people living in provinces they do not originally hail from. Who do they owe taxes to? Who owns crops grown on land in our province? Is it fair for a wood mill to charge a Metalkin more for the wood he needs for his smithy than an Evergrowth who needs the same amount of wood for a healer's hut? Does it matter where they live? It's really a very complicated issue. The innate personalities of the provinces themselves makes if very delicate as well. Take, for instance, that the Metalkin work the gold and silver but we are the ones in control of the banks. The Metalkin were the most aggressive traders before the pact, and trade with the strangers was their argument against the pact. After the pact it was deemed that, as the people chosen by the chief spirit guide, our province would control the centralized economic system – the bank."

"The bank still employs Metalkin to mint the coins and test coins for authenticity, we only handle the paperwork."

"That's a very big 'only' Princess."

"So the Metalkin do what? Exact revenge on us for this slight through trade treaties?" It sounded silly to her.

"Precisely." He looked pleased that she had grasped the concept so quickly, missing her disbelief at the idea. "They drive an aggressive deal. They will not settle any business dealings unless they feel they have the upper hand in some way. The wording of their trade agreements is tight and precise and always protects them and penalizes their trade partner. But, there is no one else, so if we want gold or iron we must trade with them."

"Then perhaps the pact was silly after all. Maybe trading with these strangers would have benefitted us all."

"Trade, yes, but we were facing an invasion, or so the histories tell us."

"But living in isolation, cut off from the rest of the world? It's so sad." She was thinking of the captain's account from before the pact. "Princess Mallory must have some amazing stories. I wonder what life is like now on the other side of the Void. Of course I don't even know what life is like outside this building."

"I hardly know either. I've spent years here studying and before that, well, my family lives in the City. Everything I know about other places I've read in a book. But someday I'll be a steward and I'll get to meet people and solve problems for them and write trade treaties."

"It sounds like an adventure. Except for the problem solving part."

"I had heard that you no longer allow an audience at court. Is it because ..?" He touched his cheek.

She turned away so the scar was hidden. Talking to him about trade treaties and ambitions she'd almost forgotten that she was different. Now she nodded. "Yes, because of the scar."

"Who makes you feel ashamed of it?"

"Everyone," she said as bitter tears filled her eyes. "The noble girls would never play with me or visit me. Their parents call my names. Their brothers think I'm ugly."

"Girls can be cruel. I grew up among a lot of girl. Girls who think they're beautiful are the worst in my experience. I could tell you a lot of stories but I'd just embarrass myself."

The tears had stopped but she didn't dare look up.

He cleared his throat. "So, uh, I would have thought you'd have a lot of experience with trade treaties and the guilds, since you're the princess."

"No," she said softly. "Most of that was set a long time ago. I only deal with the guilds when there's a problem and then I usually have my steward look up the existing trade agreement and hold everyone to the agreed upon terms. Nothing has been renegotiated in many years and I'm told it won't need to be renegotiated for several more, not unless I decide to undertake a large building project. But how many more buildings does this place need?"

"None I suppose, but I hear the main dome mosaic will need repair soon."

They talked until the sands in the hour glass ran out, and then they talked a little longer. He was laughing at something when he noticed the sands had stopped falling and his face went pale.

"How long as the hour glass been stopped?"

"Oh, I don't know. For once I wasn't paying attention."

"I'm late again. Seems to be my day for it. Thank-you for the meal Princess, it was much nicer than the food they serve in the student's dining room. I'm sorry if I offended you."

"No, not at all. Please, will you call me Vonica?"

"That is a great honour," he said with a bow that sent his hair into his eyes again. "I must return to my studies."

"I hope I will be able to visit with you again."

"So do I." He smiled and left.

Vonica finished her slice of nut bread and went straight to Master Salazar's study. She knocked and waited. She was about to knock a second time when the door opened.

When he saw her he all but threw the door open. "My apologies for keeping you waiting, Princess. Come in."

"I'm sure you're very busy."

"There's always something that requires my attention. But what can I do for you?"

"Adorjan Hearth-Glow, I want to see him again."

Salazar's eyes lit up. "Are you showing an interest, Princess?"

"No, in fact he's the first suitor to admit he has no feelings for me at all. However, he is someone I would gladly count among my friends. I want you to keep an eye on him; his desire is to be a steward. Perhaps we can point him in the direction of some lord in need of good help. He's honest, intelligent, and interesting."

"It's not really our place …"

"How many young men are awarded positions because of their last names or because of someone their father worked with? His uncle is the religious steward to Princess Rheeya Stone-Rose and he is a personal friend of mine. Why shouldn't he use those connections to find employment that will benefit him and us?"

"How will it benefit us?"

"If a friend of mine were to notice something odd he would most certainly write me and warn me of it."

"Odd? Odd how? Are you expecting trouble, Princess?"

"No. I am certain my reign will be long and boring. I just like Adorjan and I want to do something good for him."

"Of course, Princess."

Vonica nodded. "Good, I'll be going then."

"It is good to see you taking an interest in your people," Salazar said.

Vonica froze, her back stiffening. In a calm voice she said, "I have always cared about my people. I simply do not care to be a spectacle."

Johann sat drumming his fingers on the table, his head leaned against the other hand. He came to the library straight from breakfast and worked until the midday meal. After a short break he hurried back to wait for Vonica to join him after he first meeting. The candle was burning low and there was still no sign of her. He tried to shrug it off and continue his work but with every passing heart beat it was harder to concentrate. Now he sat staring at the flickering flame, his work forgotten, his mind swirling with anxious thoughts. The thoughts were so loud he didn't hear the slippered footsteps whispering up behind him.

Vonica paused, taking in the slumped and completely distracted form of her most-welcome friend. When he didn't notice her she smiled and said, "Day dreaming of something pleasant I hope?"

He jumped in his chair and twisted around. It was pure luck his elbow missed the ink. "You're –" He caught the word 'late' and replaced it with "– here."

"Of course. What are you working on today?"

"Page borders for the front plate." Again it was on the tip of his tongue to question why she was later than usual but he bit it back and focused on his work instead. It really wasn't his place to ask after all.

"They're lovely." When she was settled she said, "I'm sorry if I kept you waiting."

"I'm here all day every day," he said, trying to brush it off.

"I wish that could be my life."

"More trouble with your stewards?" He hoped the question sounded casual.

"No, actually, I lost track of time at my meeting."

"Oh, well, that's a good thing, right?"

"Very good. Master White-Cloud may even be smiling when I see him this evening."

"But you're still going to your evening meeting?"

"Oh yes. I'm only a quarter of the way through my schedule. There will be a lot more meetings yet."

Johann looked down at his work. He didn't want her to see him smiling at *that*.

10th of Cloudrise 24th Year of the 11th Rebirth
Sun Temple, Sun Temple Province

It was her day of rest again and she had spent most of the day reading across the table from Johann, the silence interspersed with short, friendly conversations. She wasn't able to really focus or enjoy the book however. Her mind had been pondering her meeting with Adorjan all week.

Finally she set her book aside and asked, "Johann, what does that book of legends say about Prophet Abner and the Metalkin?"

Johann didn't answer right away; he was focused on a rather long, curved line that had to be as close to an exact mirror image of the last one he drew as possible. The tip of the pen came off the page with a flourish and he nodded. "The Metalkin were the last province to accept Airon as the chief spirit guide," he said.

"So they were the last province Abner visited?"

"No, actually they were the first. He visited each province multiple times. I believe he went to the Metalkin seven times before he was granted an audience with their high priest or their king."

"So they were always stubborn?"

"In this case even more stubborn than the Stone Clan. I suppose that should have settled the question of which was harder, a lump of iron or a lump of stone."

"They will never stop fighting over that," Vonica said. "So what happened when Abner finally was granted his audience?"

"You have to understand, all the other provinces had bent the knee and yet the testimonies of the other kings did nothing to sway them. No amount of pressure from the kings or priests could convince them."

"They're part of the pact, they weren't left behind, and so I already know this story ends with them accepting Airon."

"Of course it does."

"I want to know what happened. How did Abner do it?"

"Abner did nothing. Airon, however, is said to have performed his greatest miracle on that day. It is second only to the pact in all our history."

"That sounds like it would have been wondrous to see."

"Frightening, actually, if you believe the tales."

"I'm not sure I would. Airon is the Sun god, a god of light and wisdom and …"

"Not all knowledge is joyous and friendly, Vonica. There are scary things on this island."

"Dark Things?"

"Yes."

"Still, Airon is good and kind. He is our protector."

"He wouldn't be a good protector if he couldn't fight for us."

"What exactly did he do?"

He found the wariness in her voice amusing. "Abner did nothing, I told you. It may have been the first recorded occurrence of him losing his temper though. Most accounts agree that there was a fair amount of yelling."

"Johann, what happened?"

He chuckled. "Okay. Abner entered Metalkin territory through the wilderness and stopped in a small village of wood cutters from Evergrowth. There were other people there but the wood cutters were the most numerous and prosperous in that town. Word had already spread among the priests of Evergrowth and Abner was welcomed joyously. He journeyed through the countryside preaching in small towns of farmers and carpenters. He did no miracles in those days for he had the full backing of the priests of Evergrowth and Animal People. But the Metalkin priests in those villages sent word back to their high priest and the king."

"What did the average Metalkin think? Obviously the priests were upset but what about the blacksmiths? Or the gold smiths?"

"Who can say? History seems wholly uninterested in the inner thoughts of the blacksmiths."

"But you said the woodcutters greeted him joyously."

"Only because the priests of Evergrowth had already done the hard work. Who knows how the wood cutters and farmers first reacted. But the priests had already answered questions, offered assurances, and uttered threats."

"Threats?" she scoffed.

"Short of miracles, threats are the most effective way to convert people."

"I've never heard High Priest Balder ever speak an unkind word let alone a threat!"

"You're not one of his priests, or a wayward follower."

"You've changed the subject. What happened in the Metalkin province?"

"To be fair it was you who side tracked me. Still, I'll tell you what happened. You have to understand, it didn't just happen in the Metalkin Province – it happened to the whole island."

"Then why isn't it common knowledge?"

"It's legend, there's no proof it ever happened. And it's fairly unbelievable. Would you believe it possible to blacken the sky?"

"You mean thunder clouds? Or night time?"

"No, and not quite."

"Then how?"

"It's a miracle, Vonica, there is no explanation."

She smiled at him.

"What?"

"Nothing. Tell me the whole story. When did the miracle happen? What was the reaction?"

"Oh, everyone agrees that the reaction was mass panic and complete hysteria. The rest, well, it is just legend, there are many versions."

"Tell me the best version."

Now he smiled at her. "Abner returned to the province of the Metalkin and eventually his preaching was noticed by the religious authorities. It was decided among the priests of the Metalkin that it was time to deal with what they labelled heresy."

"But everyone else believed it."

"So it was a pervasive heresy, all the more reason to put an end to it. Until this point each province had been separate and the Metalkin priests and king feared losing their independence. The priests went to the king and convinced him that Abner was a very serious threat to their way of life, their taxes, and their freedom. The king wasn't hard to convince and he issued an order for Abner's arrest."

"That's horrible."

"If it's true."

"Why would someone make it up?"

"When Abner finally stood before the mighty Metalkin king he was a prisoner in chains, the lowest of the low against the highest of the high. They meant to humiliate him. He just continued preaching and praying. He had an answer to every one of their questions. Finally they asked for proof. 'We've stripped you of your tricks. You will never be able to prove your lies now. Still we will give you the chance. Prove the mightiness of Airon now.' But Abner replied, 'I can't, I never could, but Airon can, and he will.' Of course they didn't believe him until a shadow fell across the land. They rushed outside to see a great black shadow rolling across the face of the sun, so thick it hid all the light.

"When only the thinnest ring of light remained around the edge of the shadow and the whole island sat in darkness the king of the Metalkin finally bent the knee to Airon. He had to order his priests to kneel but finally everyone came until the guidance of Airon."

"Just like that?"

"If you saw the sun turn black and night fall at midday I'm sure you would give up your doubts fairly quickly. Any lingering doubts were silenced. And then all these stories became the tedious sermons of history. The priesthoods were restructured. Treaties were signed. New religious texts were written and distributed. Philosophers had much to debate. A time of peace and balance swept the land and we remained, for the most part, prosperous until the threat of the strangers from beyond the sea. That of course prompted the pact."

"I wish I could be a part of something so memorable that legends grow from my deeds."

"There are legends about the first princesses already and you're only the eleventh rebirth. In a few generations the commoners will be telling stories about you around their fires on cold winter nights."

"I can guess what they'll be saying about me." All the joy and delight went out of her voice.

"Stop. That's not the first thing everyone sees."

She nodded, afraid her voice would crack if she spoke.

"I've entertained you with my stories. Maybe you will entertain me with one."

The request caught her by surprise and she stammered, "But you're so talented at telling stories."

"A talent that can be learned with practice."

"You know much better stories than I do."

"Why don't you tell me about your suitor the other day, the one whom you favoured with more than an hour of your time? I'm curious about the one man you've spoken favourably of in this whole process."

"I wasn't late just because of him. I also had to stop and talk to my steward."

"At least tell me what you talked about for the hour so I know what stories to tell you next time."

"Oh, well, that's easy. We talked about the Metalkin."

He looked at her a moment and then laughed. "And so I have already told you the legend of the Metalkin. Seems you will have to tell me another story then. One from your childhood perhaps?"

Relieved at not having to talk about Adorjan in front of Johann she smiled. "I think I know just the story about four girls and some frogs."

17th of Cloudrise 24th Year of the 11th Rebirth
Sun Temple, Sun Temple Province

Vonica walked through the library feeling a little anxious. She'd brought her own candle today in a brass holder and had lit it from the torch at the doors. As she hurried to the table the flame flickered and strained. *Please let him be there today.* She chanted the thought over and over until it became a prayer.

She'd come the day before between meetings as always only to be greeted by a dark alcove and an empty table. She'd stayed as long as she dared, waiting, hoping, as doubts crept through her mind, chased by shaky reassurances that he was not mad at her.

Through the shelves Vonica saw the soft, warm glow of candlelight.

He had his back to the opening in the shelves, as always. He had two candles on the table between the glass bottles of coloured ink. He was hunched over his work, his quill moving in slow, deliberate, sweeping strokes.

Her breath caught in her throat. *What if he's mad at me? What if he doesn't want me here?* The doubts spoiled her excitement and she approached cautiously.

Johann was working on a particularly detailed corner of roses when something moved on the edge of his vision. He looked up, smiled, and set the quill back in the bottle of red ink. "You're early this morning, did you even attend service?"

"I did yes. And you're late."

"I'm here before you," he said.

"A whole day late."

His cheeks flushed slightly. "Oh, yes, about that. I'm sorry. Master Bright-Quill needed to speak with me and I knew you had meetings so I agreed. But then he went on and on with suggestions and new requirements and I knew I'd be late but really I had no choice but to listen."

"I wasn't sure you'd be back today."

"And many more days to come. It seems that Master Bright-Quill mentioned my work to another Master Scholar and now he wants me to illuminate a manuscript for him as well."

"While I missed our usual time together that is wonderful news."

"You would think so."

"Why? What isn't good about this?"

"Well, it's just that this new project is a rather lengthy compendium."

Wariness stilled her excitement for him. "A compendium of what, exactly?"

"Legends."

"Oh dear." She giggled. She couldn't help it. She put a hand over her mouth to hide the smile and held her breath.

"Yes, that's putting it mildly. This is why Master Bright-Quill had so many suggestions and additions. It will not be several months at least before I can begin the second project."

"At least you have work. I was worried."

"I'm sorry. I didn't know how to get a message to you. I wasn't sure a message from an illuminator would reach you. And by the time I knew this meeting was going to go so late there really wasn't much time to send a message."

"Johann, it's all right. You're all right so now I have nothing to worry about."

21st of Cloudrise 24th Year of the 11th Rebirth
Sun Temple, Sun Temple Province

Antony White-Cloud barged into Salazar's room just as a servant girl was setting out a meal on the round wooden table. His sudden appearance startled her and she dropped a tray's cover. It clattered loudly on the floor. She quickly bent to retrieve it. "I'm sorry my lords."

"It's nothing," Salazar said to her then turned to his fellow steward. "Would you care for a meal? I can have more sent up."

"No."

Salazar nodded and dismissed the girl. When she was gone Antony dropped into an empty chair. "I don't understand. Something is wrong."

"I will offer you what council I can old friend."

"The nobles are complaining louder than ever. They say the meetings are taking too long, that their daughters are waiting for suitors who will not come to call until the princess is wed."

"She's missed fewer meetings this week."

"She must meet them two at a time, and she must hold more meetings during the day. The nobles are insisting."

"We don't serve the noble families. We serve Princess Vonica and so do they."

"She made an agreement, Salazar, and she's still skipping meetings!"

"I'm confident she will find her prince very soon."

"The only man she's moved to the front of the list blatantly said he was not her prince. She's asked for a dozen men to be removed from the list completely."

"Which you haven't done."

"She could be wrong."

"No princess has been wrong before. And you have to admit it will be easier for her to find her prince if she shortens the list."

"We're holding the ball."

"Antony, be patient with her. She is changing by the day, I can feel it. She must learn to ignore her scar, to live with it, to love herself. If we push her now she'll retreat into fear again."

"If we don't push her we'll have a revolt on our hands."

"The nobles won't take up arms against her because it took six months instead of two. You're overreacting."

"You're not taking this seriously enough."

Salazar had been trying to stay calm and reasonable. He set his fork down on the table, hard, and found his anger slipping into his voice. "Do not doubt my devotion to the princess, or to this province. Mallory is the only princess who has found her prince. Vonica will not be the last, I assure you of that." He sighed. "She is growing and maturing right now, she is becoming more confident. If we betray her trust …"

"Betray her? What accusations are you making?"

"None. Antony, if you break your word she will retreat into herself again. She must be able to trust us or she will never learn to trust anyone else."

"I'm making the arrangements for the ball. I already notified the other stewards in the other provinces. If their girls are being difficult too then …"

"Vonica will not allow this."

"I'm not giving her a choice."

Salazar picked up his fork. "You are making a very serious mistake old friend."

Vonica was humming as she ran her brush through her hair. Mary had gone to fetch more tea and would be back any moment to put her hair up for the day. When she came in she smiled. "I haven't heard you humming since before our trip to Golden Hall. What has you in such a good mood?"

"I finished a wonderful book last night."

"Oh? All this over a book?"

"Why? Shouldn't I be happy?"

"I'm glad you are happy. I was hoping for more joyous news."

"Please. I don't want to talk about that, not when the morning is so lovely."

"Well, you'd best change your mind about that, Princess. Master White-Cloud has requested your presence before court this morning."

"Did he mention what the meeting concerned?"

"No. But he was not humming."

"I see. Thank-you. Best pull out one of the nicer day dresses then."

"Yes, Princess."

Vonica took a deep breath before knocking on the study door. "Master White-Cloud, you requested my presence?"

The door opened. "Ah, Princess. Thank-you for agreeing to see me this morning. Come in. I will make this quick so we are not late for court."

"It must be important if it could not wait until after court."

"Very important. I wish to speak with you about your suitors."

"What about my suitors?"

"I am going to begin planning the ball."

"What? You can't hold a ball without my permission."

"I didn't come to ask your permission, Princess. I came only to keep you informed. We will begin preparations for the ball tomorrow."

Antony expected shouting, he expected hysterics, and he expected that, in the end, she would concede to his age and his wisdom and agree to the ball. What he wasn't ready for was the way she straightened her posture and met his gaze.

"If you begin planning this ball then I will no longer attend the scheduled meetings with the suitors."

"Princess, I must …"

"We had a deal, Master White-Cloud. By planning this ball you are releasing me from my end of the deal."

"The noble families will not be pleased."

"You can tell them it was their impatience, and yours, that brought this about."

Changing indeed, Antony thought. *But not necessarily for the best.* He bowed. "As you say Princess."

30th of Cloudrise 24th Year of the 11th Rebirth
Sun Temple, Sun Temple Province

Vonica sighed and closed the book she was reading.

"Finished already?" Johann filled in yet another red rose petal and glanced up at her.

"It wasn't a long book, but it was very interesting."

"Do you want me to recommend another one?"

"My eyes could use a rest. Tell me a story."

"I think you know every story about Abner that I know by now."

"Then tell me a different story. Tell me about your home."

"Well I have an older brother, Tullius, and a younger sister named Ioanna."

"Do you miss them?"

"I left home fourteen years ago. I've been home a half dozen times in those years. My parents visit for Holy Week every few years. That's enough for me. I suppose I could do with seeing my sister more. I'm surprised she hasn't convinced my father to send her here."

"I've seen the other princesses twice in the last twelve years. I miss them terribly."

"We weren't close. My brother was busy swinging a sword with my father and my sister was learning all about managing a household from my mother, even at eight years old. So when a scholar came from the capital and requested I come here for schooling I think the arrangement made everyone happy."

"So this is your home?"

"It is and it isn't. I'm happy here, sure, but I spent the first ten years of my life there. I miss the library there and sitting in from of the fire in the winter with a long book."

"So you grew up in a keep?"

"You caught me."

She laughed, her eyes twinkling in the candlelight.

"I grew up in a keep in the company of scholars and was happiest when I could draw. I drew pictures in the dirt with my sparring sword and my brother knocked me in the dirt every time."

"You're very good you know."

"I almost wound up in a builder's guild. I like detail. But when I arrived here the guild master said they'd already taken on new apprentices."

"But now you're stuck here. If you had joined the builder's guild you could have moved anywhere on the Isle of Light."

"I still could. There's a book bindery guild in all five capital cities and each one employs several illuminators, even if they are technically Evergrowth guilds."

"So why haven't you joined one?"

"None of them have offered me a position."

"Then they haven't seen your work."

"They likely have. My name isn't on any of it."

"What?"

"Master Agoston Bright-Quill will have his name on this book, credited as the author and researcher, and my name will not appear anywhere on it."

"That doesn't seem right."

He shrugged. "Apparently that's the way it's always been. And good luck getting the Scholars to change."

"I could decree a change."

"They'll probably ignore it. There's a law you know, about not meddling in academic affairs. Something about maintaining independence and freedom from bias and corruption."

"But I'm the Princess."

"Not every rule is fair or just."

"What they're doing to you isn't fair or just."

"Are you really upset by it?"

"Yes."

"I'm not."

She blinked at him. "You're not?"

"I like living here. I love this library and all its dusty ancient books. I have a reputation for being slow and meticulous but really I rush most of the work so I can read. I have friends, a nice room, and decent food. I like the garden and the temple. And I like spending time with you."

"Really? I'm not slowing you down too much?"

"No. Far from it. You are my muse, my inspiration."

She looked away, blushing.

"In fact, there's something I want to tell you."

"Yes."

A bell sounded in the distance and she sat up straight. "Is that the dinner bell already?"

He nodded.

"I'm late!" She sprang out of her chair. "I'm sorry. I have to go. I have guests for dinner."

"I thought you were done meeting suitors."

"I was. I am. This is for the ball. Master White-Cloud says it's important. I'm sorry. You'll tell me next time, won't you?"

"Of course."

"It may be a few days before I can slip away again."

"I'll be here." As he watched her hurry away the smile dropped from his face. He packed up his work. He would put it away and find dinner, maybe spend the evening working on his current painting, and tomorrow he would be back, waiting on the slim chance that Vonica would be able to slip away."

3rd of Thornrise 24th Year of the 11th Rebirth
Sun Temple, Sun Temple Province

Lately court has been full of the most boring complaints, Vonica thought. *It's like Master White-Cloud has requested extra petitioners just to keep me busy.* She glanced at Antony but his attention was on the petitioner. They were the only three people in the room. All guards were posted outside the doors, as usual, and Vonica had actually won the fight to keep the nobles off the observation benches.

After sending this petitioner on his way she turned to Antony again. "How many more today?"

"Not too many, Princess. You are not deliberating over long on any of the cases so though it was a lengthy list it shouldn't take much time."

That's because it's all been petty and boring, she thought but she knew better than to say the thought out loud. "Call in the next petitioner. I'm ready."

Master White-Cloud was correct, there were in fact only four more petitioners and all of them simple matters. Vonica stretched. "If that's everything for today?"

"You haven't been to your lessons in over a month."

"I've been in the library studying the Prophet Abner and …"

There was a commotion outside the door. Antony started down the steps. Before he could reach the door it burst open and a bedraggled man in peasant's garb stumbled in. A guard caught his shoulder, saving him from a fall.

"I'm sorry, Princess. We'll remove him at once."

A second guard stepped up and grabbed the man's arm.

"Please! I must speak with the princess, I must!"

"He's not on the list, it can wait until tomorrow," Antony said.

"No, please, I have a message for the princess."

"A message? From whom?" Vonica said.

"Lord Sun-Song."

"And why didn't Lord Sun-Song just send a bird?" Antony shook his head and scoffed. He waved at the guards. "Take him away."

"No! Please. There was a fire. Please. It spread to the eyrie. Please. We need help."

"Let him pass," Vonica said. "Bring me the letter."

The writing was messy and smudged but the seal was intact.

"What news?" Antony prompted.

"Fire," Vonica said, still reading. Some of the words were hard to decipher. "They are requesting stone masons, carpenters, and healers. They also need hawks as theirs are either injured or escaped."

"I'll send letters to the necessary guilds," Antony said.

"Give this man a meal before you send him on his way," Vonica said. She smiled at the man. "Tell your lord that help is coming."

"Thank-you," he said. He went out with the guards, no longer fighting them.

"You will be attending lessons again," Antony said.

"No, I have other things to take care of. Excuse me."

The nook in the library was dark but Vonica had her own candle. She sat at the table and reread the letter, waiting for Johann. He'd been late before though on one occasion he had failed to show. She perused the shelves and flipped through a few books. She reread the letter again. The bell for the midday meal sounded. Her candle flickered and burned low.

She lifted her head from her arms. Her candle had gone out. There were voices from somewhere in the library so it couldn't be too late. She stretched.

If he's not here by now then he's not coming. Master Bright-Quill must have kept him busy today. I will ask his opinion on this matter tomorrow.

4th of Thornrise 24th Year of the 11th Rebirth
Sun-Song Estate, Sun Temple Province

Johann did not return home often. His work at the library kept him busy and content but more than that the capital felt like home in a way home never had, and now he knew why. That's what he'd been trying to tell Vonica the last time he'd seen her.

He handed his horse over to a stable boy he didn't recognize and slung his bag over his shoulder. Octavian Gold-Hearth, his father's steward, was waiting for him at the front door.

"Master Johann. I wasn't sure you would come. Your room has been prepared."

"My thanks. How is everyone faring?"

"You saw the damage on your way through the village?"

"Some of it."

"They are distressed."

"Yes, of course."

"I'll tell your father you've arrived."

"Thank-you." Johann watched Octavian leave, his hands behind his back. *That man has a personality colder than a winter wind.* He shook his head.

As he made his way through the halls the servants ignored him. He wasn't dressed like a lord's son, or even like a visiting scholar, and he'd been away for more than a year. He appreciated the anonymity as it gave him privacy. All that would change after he met with his father and the serving staff passed along word of his return. Then it would be bowing and constant questions. Did he need anything? Was he hungry? Did he have errands he needed run? Questions and more questions until he chased them away and earned a reproach from his mother. He unpacked his clothes into the familiar wardrobe.

Johann retied his hair and put away his riding clothes. He changed into his robe and put on the brown sash that marked him a scholar. Master Scholars had gold trim on their brown sashes. Octavian's sash was green with no brown trim or embroidery which meant he was a steward but not a full scholar. He did have his house crest embroidered on the sash, just above the hip, in exquisite detail.

He was expecting his parents so he was surprised when he entered the study and was greeted by his father and his brother. "Father, Tullius. Where's Mother?"

"She's conferring with the healers who arrived shortly before you did to assist with those injured in the fire. You had a safe journey?"

"Yes sir."

"Your brother will be going back with you."

"Oh?" Johann eyed his brother. Tullius visited the capital even less than Johann visited home. "What's the occasion?"

"The royal ball of course," Tullius said. "The invitation hasn't arrived yet but as one of her suitors I will, of course, receive one."

"I'd have thought you'd be in the capital already."

"I was preparing to leave when the message came that the meetings were cancelled. Two dozen lucky men got to spend time alone with her. They were obviously the wrong men though."

"I agree."

"Have you met her? The princess?"

Johann fidgeted. "You know your meeting was to be before mine."

"We'll meet her at the ball then."

"How bad was the fire?" Johann said, turning back to his father and safer subjects.

"Lost the black smith shop, forge, and house. Just the stone from the forge left. Also lost half a dozen houses, including one of the teachers'. It scorched about three acres of farm land, burned down two barns, and a lot of fencing. The animals survived. Damaged the gate and spread to the stables and the eyrie. All the damn birds got loose. Four people are dead. Another twelve are wounded but only two are serious. Fortunately it is spring and we have nearly half the year to rebuild before the snows come. Healers have already arrived from the capital with news that men are on their way to help. They're also sending birds and supplies."

"It's good we had a wet spring," Tullius said. "Or else we could have lost more farm land."

"I'm glad you chose to keep me informed but I don't see why you requested I return home." The letter he'd received wasn't worded as a request, it was a demand. "I don't know how much help I can be."

"Nonsense. I'll need you to help Master Gold-Heart with the complaints and requests coming in. You know how to keep records and such."

"And such, yes."

"There are – other – reasons but we shall speak on that later. For now why don't you go with Tullius? He can show you the extent of the damage and the work requirements."

"I've spent the entire day on the road and I've already changed from my riding clothes."

"Then change back. I'll see you both for dinner at the usual time." Lord Sun-Song waved them away.

"Be quick," Tullius said as they went out of the study. "I'll meet you by what's left of the stable."

It was tempting to bar the door and simply not go but his father would find out and it would result in a lecture at dinner.

Just leave, a part of him whispered. *Go back to the capital and the library and Vonica. You left without warning or even a note. But whom could you trust to deliver it? Father made his summons sound so urgent. Damn him.*

Back in his dirty clothes he joined his brother and together they rode down to the village. Large tents were being set up over the charred remains of a field.

"The healers," Tullius said, though from the number of slender men and women with light brown hair milling about and stirring great cauldrons over fires it was mostly self-evident.

They finally stopped at a pile of charred rubble where the black smith shop should have been. The smith himself, a large, black-haired man in filthy clothes, was busy shovelling away ashes.

Johann had fond memories of the old smith, one Jael Black. He had been large too; his tree-trunk arms the result of long hours spent hammering out plows and horse shoes, and his hands nearly as tough as his leather apron. Jael's hair had already shown grey at the temples when Johann was just a boy. He'd been too interested in the forge and all its workings for his father's liking but Jael had indulged him.

This new smith was younger than Jael, but still older than Tullius. The two boys helping him clear rubble had the same thick black hair and iron-hard eyes. They were most likely his sons, and apprentices.

Tullius dismounted in front of the ruins. "Hail, Jon!"

He looked up, frowning. "Master Sun-Song, we are quite busy. There is much cleaning we have to do before we rebuild."

"We won't interrupt. I wanted my brother to see where the fire started."

'I', not 'my father', as though it were his idea. He always was the little lord. Johann forced a smile. "I am sorry for your loss. I hope none of your family was hurt."

"So this is the boy. We are all safe and well, my thanks for your concern. The rest of the village holds us responsible for the lives lost."

"We don't know what started the fire," Tullius said. "We may never know." Leading his horse he said, "Come, there is more to see."

5th of Thornrise 24th Year of the 11th Rebirth
Sun Temple, Sun Temple Province

Vonica returned from the library and rang for Mary. "I wasn't expecting you back this morning, Princess."

"Bring me tea, please. And I'll have the midday meal here. I'm behind on my correspondence. I'll be working at my desk for most of the day."

"Of course." She curtsied and hurried out.

The first dozen letters were quarterly reports from various estates and guilds across the province. One of the benefits of ruling the smallest province on a small island nation was that Vonica had met every ruling noble and every guild leader serving under her. She received letters from each of them four times per year, more often if there was a problem. Past princesses had shared an even closer bond with the lords and ladies and a few wrote to her with a familiarity born of a past friendship. Sometimes Vonica wished she could remember her past lives.

She finished her tea and took a short stroll around her garden to stretch her legs and rest her mind. The first scroll she picked up when she returned to her desk bore a red wax seal with the emblem of a square-cut gem adorned with a rose in bloom. She broke the seal and unrolled the letter from Princess Mallory Jewel-Rose.

Dear Vonica Bright-Rose, 11th Rebirth of the Sun Temple Princess, Keeper of the Pact, and Daughter of the Sun,

I've not had many occasions to write to you and even fewer to meet you in person. I sincerely hope I didn't forget any titles. This is all still a little bewildering to me. I am writing at the request of Princess Rheeya Stone-Rose as there seems to be trouble in her province and trouble has a tendency to spread. I may be new to the Isle of Light but even where I am from I have found this to be true.

I'm not sure what Rheeya has told you so I think it's best I fill you in so you are aware of the extent of the problem. The mine collapse in Rheeya's province appears to be the fault of one Jared Iron-Smith, an Iron Guild representative to the Stone Clan province. Former Iron Guild representative I should say. Rheeya has stripped him of his position within her province and I have stripped him of both his title and position here.

Rheeya has requested that I do a full inquiry into the Iron Guild at the very least and recommends that I extend this to all the guilds. I completely agree with this recommendation and wish to take this one step further.

This letter serves as permission from me to request and examine all records from the Metalkin guilds operating within your province. It is my sincerest hope that you find nothing amiss. In the event that you do find something do not hesitate to report it to me and take any other disciplinary actions you deem fit. I must know how far this problem reaches.

I have been busy learning about this world and my role in it and I have been told that we princesses are traditionally discouraged from travelling but I hope that I will get the chance to see you again. Perhaps this time we will have more of a chance to talk with each other. I understand that your people are the keepers of the island's history. Master Etemaad Golden-Heart has been helpful, of course, more helpful than Master Conrad Silver-Crest, but there are questions neither wishes to answer. Perhaps you can shed more light on them.

Princess Mallory Brock Jewel-Rose, Princess of the Metalkin

Vonica pulled out the quarterly report from the Merchant Bank in Stones Shore and the soot smudged scroll from the Lord Sun-Song. Halfway down she found the line: "At this time it is believed that the fire originated at the black smith shop."

She glanced at the next letter. "Princess Rheeya reopened an account for the widow of a guard against protests from Lord Bartlet Golden-Heart."

It has to be coincidence.

Even if the fire was an accident, and even if the matter of the widow's account was just a misunderstanding that occurred when Bartlet took over the Stones Shore bank from his father, Mallory's concerns were very real and very serious. She had been avoiding her stewards as much as possible since Antony had made the decision to plan the ball but now she would need their advice on how and when to proceed.

She met servant at the door. "Oh, Princess, I have your tray here."

Vonica took a step back. "Is it midday already?"

"Yes, M'Lady. Do you still want to eat?"

"Yes, bring it in. And find Master White-Cloud and Master Sun-Wise. I must speak with them as soon as they are free."

"Yes Princess."

Vonica barely had time to finish eating before her stewards were at her door. She handed them Mallory's letter and let them read while she finished her tea.

"This is a serious matter," she said, setting her cup down. "We need to respond quickly."

"Respond to what, Princess? We have no control over what happens in Stone Clan territory and no one in our guilds is implicated in this," Antony said. He looked to Salazar for support.

Salazar shrugged. "It is Vonica's duty to uphold the balance of the pact within this province. Improper business practices can threaten that."

"Nonsense," Antony said. "I've not heard one complaint from the noble families in a decade."

"And perhaps she'll find nothing. It's still in everyone's best interest for her to look into the matter," Salazar replied.

"Everyone? Our province is home to some of the wealthiest guild representatives on the Isle of Light. They employ tutors, artists, accountants, and stewards, from among our people. It would be in the best interest of those people if their employers did not feel that their privacy was being invaded. Not to mention that you are threatening their position and station."

"Their position and station does not give them permission to threaten the balance of the pact."

"Salazar, you are exaggerating the problem to the point of the ridiculous."

"Enough," Vonica said. "Since the two of you cannot agree I will seek out other opinions before making my decision. I need to speak to a specific scholar."

"Of course Princess," Salazar said. "Who may I fetch for you?"

"His name is Johann and he is in the employ of Master Agoston Bright-Quill."

"Employ?" Antony said. "In what capacity?"

Vonica looked down at her hands. "An illuminator."

"You wish to consult an artist?"

But Salazar stood and bowed. "I shall find him for you at once. Come, Master White-Cloud, our princess has work to do."

Still spluttering Antony followed Salazar out.

Vonica let out a deep breath and went out to her garden. Near the center was a large rose bush that was currently covered in fat

85

buds. Any day now they would begin to open and set the bush afire until almost all the dark green leaves were hidden. It was one of her favourite spots. Here she felt grounded, confident.

Would Johann like this spot as much as I do? She had never seen him outside of the library. *Will he come?* She reached out to touch one fragile bud. Her fingers were trembling.

She was pacing by the time the knock came at the door. The sound made her jump. "Come in." She smoothed her skirt and looked up, smiling. "Oh, Mary."

"Pardon me, Princess. I've brought Master Bright-Quill to see you."

"Of course, show him in."

Mary opened the door wide to let an imposing middle-aged man into the room. He bowed with a wide sweep of his arm. His robe billowed around him. "Princess Vonica, it is a great honour to stand before you."

"And I am honoured to meet you. I have had the privilege of viewing your latest collection of history and myth."

"My thanks. I understand you are searching for Master Sun-Song."

"Sun-Song? You mean Johann?"

"Yes, Princess. He was called away two days ago on urgent business."

"I can guess what that business might be," Vonica murmured. "My thanks for coming to tell me."

"Of course. Uh, is it possible that I might be of service to you?"

"No. It was not a scholarly matter."

"Then I will take my leave."

Everything made sense now, at least concerning Johann's absence. There was still the matter of Mallory's letter and what to do about it. "Mary, there is someone else I need to speak to."

"Who, M'Lady?"

"Adorjan Hearth-Glow."

He was quicker to respond and greeted her with a much less flourished bow. "I never thought I would receive a summons to your private wing."

"I did tell you that I looked forward to a friendship with you, did I not?"

"You did. Did you consider how this will appear to the other noble houses?"

"I don't much care how they choose to view this. At this point you may be the only one I trust."

"That is high praise, of course, but at the same time disconcerting. I suppose we'd best get down to business then."

She invited him to her desk with a gesture. She pulled out the scroll from Mallory and handed it to him. In the silence while he read she called for Mary and had her bring tea and cakes for two. When he finished he accepted a cup from her and sipped.

"You're frowning," she said. "Then it is serious."

"Of course it's serious. Tell me, instinctively, what did you feel needed to be done?"

"A full record review of Metalkin guilds, at the very least. And any connected guild if anything suspicious arises."

"That's the reaction I would expect from a concerned princess. Why haven't you done it yet?"

"Because I am young and sometimes our instinctive need to defend at all costs benefits from wisdom and experience."

"In other words, you spoke to your stewards."

"Of course. I'm one person; I cannot see every possible outcome of my actions. I'm supposed to ask for their advice. I thought they would help me plan out the best way to get the job done. They should have told me how to word my requests and who to address them to. I want to avoid insult but I must do what's right for my people. Now I feel like all my instincts were wrong."

"As far as I'm concerned your stewards are wrong."

"But just the one," Vonica said. "Master Sun-Wise did try to agree with me. It's all so confusing. My two stewards never seem to agree on anything. I don't know who to listen to."

"You are the chosen one of Airon, the keeper of the pact, and our sacred defender. Say a prayer and do whatever it is that Airon puts in your heart."

"It can't be that easy."

"Why not? Princess, you are self-conscious of your scar, whether you should be or not, but that does not affect your ability to think." He blushed. "My apologies, Princess. It is not my place to chastise you. Forgive me for my outburst."

"There's nothing to forgive," she said, her voice distant. She pulled her thoughts back from self-contemplation to the task at hand. "You'll help me write the letters."

"Princess, I'm not politician. I have no experience with correct political matters."

"You studied the Metalkin; you know more about them than anyone else I know. And you want to be a steward so consider this your practical education."

"Yes, of course Princess. Let's begin."

"What is this?"

Vonica looked up from her dinner and smiled. "Ah, Master White-Cloud, won't you join us?"

Antony's gaze snapped over as he noticed Adorjan for the first time since storming in, scroll in hand. He straightened and cleared his throat. "My apologies, I didn't realize you were dining with a suitor."

"I'm not; I'm dining with a friend. Please, sit." She gestured to an open seat.

Antony sat as servants brought him a place setting. "You are a member of the Hearth-Glow family if I'm not mistaken."

"You are correct, and I am impressed. Most people say I favour my mother. Adorjan Hearth-Glow. My uncle is Alessandro Hearth-Glow, the current steward to Princess Rheeya Stone-Rose."

"Yes, of course. I studied with him. You are on the list of suitors, correct?"

"Was. I've removed my name. I feel no soul connection or romantic attraction to Princess Vonica. Why should I waste her time, or yours?"

"And yet you are here."

"He's here at my request. I needed assistance and recalled Adorjan was studying the very issue, or at least something closely related."

"It is my job to assist you."

"Yes. I also asked for your advice on this matter."

"And then chose to ignore it."

"I had to ignore you or Master Salazar as the two of you disagreed. I asked for a third opinion and did what I thought was best for my people."

"This!" He waved the scroll. "You are going to insult a lot of people with this outrage."

"I cannot allow anyone to use the threat of wounded pride to tie my hands. If something is wrong I need to know. If nothing is wrong I will thank everyone for their cooperation and apologize for inconveniencing them."

"When?"

"Excuse me?"

"When will you issue this apology?"

"I assume I will issue it when the investigation is complete and if no issues arise in the meanwhile."

"You will issue it in person, I insist upon that."

"We shall see if it is even necessary."

Antony hmphed. "Since you are set on this foolhardy course I will leave you so I may prepare for the complaints that are bound to arrive on my desk. I will see you tomorrow, Princess, so we may begin planning the main program for the ball. We will need to move quickly before the noble families lose patience."

"It will have to wait."

Antony stopped halfway to the door. "Wait? You are the one who claims to be putting the needs of your people first and yet you delay in finding your prince? This is the most important task that you have! Already there are reports of Dark Things becoming bolder in the southern parts of the Stone Clan province, the Northern Coast, and the North Woods of the Evergrowth province, which is right on our border. They will spread! Even Mallory was attacked on her journey to the Isle of Light. Twenty four years ago when you and the others were brought over that never would have happened. The pact was strong then!"

"The marriage of the princesses is not the only thing that affects the pact," Adorjan said.

"I do not need to be lectured on theology by a man who hasn't even earned the title of Master Scholar!" He stormed out, the scroll now crushed in his fist.

"He didn't eat," Vonica mused, her eyes on Antony's empty plate.

"Is every day like this for you?"

"No," Vonica said. "I usually don't talk back like that. I can't believe I did that. Masters White-Cloud and Sun-Wise have been my advisors since I was twelve years old. They ran this province when I was too young."

"If that is their normal way of speaking to you then it is time you stood up to them."

"No, that isn't normal, really. It's only been like this since I returned from Golden Hall."

Adorjan nodded. "There has always been some competition between provinces to be first, or at least not last, to see their princess wed. Our province has never been last and that puts pressure on your stewards. But that does not give them the right to bully you like this."

"It's fine. We're all stressed. I have a duty. I have to find my prince. But talking to people and attending balls makes me feel sick. I'm failing everyone."

"No, I think they are failing you."

6th of Thornrise 24th Year of the 11th Rebirth
Sun Temple, Sun Temple Province

Vonica returned from court and eyed the letters waiting on her desk with a mixture of excitement and grim determination. She honestly had not expected so many responses so soon. Even though she'd spent the morning sitting down she hurried to her desk and settled into the chair. She opened the first, closed with the seal of the Silver Guild, and found not the requested information or even an invitation to visit the guild and see the records in person, but a flat refusal and condescending admonishment.

"You overstep your rights."

"You suggest without evidence that we are breaking your laws."

"We've come to expect more courteous behaviour from our leaders and rulers than you have shown."

Frowning she opened the next letter, this time from the Jeweler's Guild, and found more of the same. Each letter in turn bore a strict, and barely polite, refusal accompanied by thinly veiled insults to the quality of her manners and threats to report her requests to Princess Mallory. By the time she reached the last letter her hands were trembling and her chest was tight.

This final letter bore the seal of the Merchant's Bank. Though they worked closely with the Metalkin guilds and employed many Metalkin the bank was overseen by men of the Sun Temple Province, men who owed their allegiance directly to her.

Surely they will co-operate. At least I will have somewhere to start.

The letter did not contain an outright refusal, nor did it contain the requested information. Instead it contained an apology.

"Master Maceo Heart-Flame, our archivist and record keeper, passed away recently. His death was very sudden and came as a sorrowful surprise to us all. His passing has left the archives in a state of disarray. We are in the process of selecting a new archivist. As soon as possible we will forward him your request and he will provide you with the records you require as promptly as possible. As for the current accounts you requested, those will be forthcoming soon. Many of our clerks and accountants are either grieving the loss of Master Heart-Flame or involved in the selection process. With the fire at the Sun-Song estate and the current upheaval in the Stone Clan territory we find we are understaffed and overworked."

Vonica dropped the letter on the desk, put her head down on her arms, and broke down crying.

There was a knock on the door. Vonica dried her eyes and blew her nose before calling, "Come in."

Master Sun-Wise entered and bowed. "Good morning, Princess. I hope I am not interrupting." He frowned. "Is everything all right?"

"Yes, fine."

He nodded, still frowning. "I've spent yesterday evening and this morning recording anything that may be of assistance to you during your investigation. I'm afraid it's not much but if I think of anything else of course I will let you know."

Vonica took the offered scrolls. "You're the only one, it seems. Not one of the guilds will cooperate."

"There are laws, regulations …"

"Master White-Cloud is against this investigation. Forcing him to help will turn into a battle and he will use it to force me to concede many points on the matter of the royal ball in exchange for his help in this."

"Princess, have a seat. You look distressed."

My eyes must be red still from the crying. She sat by the hearth and waited.

"Princess, when your predecessor chose Antony and I to train to be your stewards thirty-five years ago everything was different. We had enjoyed nearly sixty years of peace and prosperity. Trade was strong. No one had seen a Dark Thing in decades. Antony and I were young, idealistic, and full of hope. The last Vonica, she was a beacon. Strong and intense yet calm, steadying. The stewards who had raised her had already retired and the replacements were stewards in name only. She ruled almost alone, save for the aid of her prince. Her stewards trained us. I was taught mostly how to help you navigate your dealings with the church and to teach you the various formal phrases. Antony was taught about the political dealings of the noble houses and how to help you avoid insulting them."

"Whose job was it to make sure I found my prince?"

"Ah, well, that was always a bone of contention between us. Since your soul bond is a critical part of your pact with Airon it is a religious matter. However, with each rebirth the courtship process becomes more ritualized and formal and has very much become entwined with the politics of the noble houses."

"Can I choose a side? Can I please put you in charge so Antony can no longer plan a royal ball I don't want to attend?"

"Well now, that's where part of the problem lies. You see, your past incarnations, they enjoyed people. They hosted balls and dinners. They invited people to dinner. Because you have always had a quiet nature and because of your scar you do not go out of your way to meet people the way they did."

"I don't want to meet people the way they did and I hate the forced dinners and I do not want to go to a royal ball so everyone can stare at me and snicker at me."

"We have to provide you with opportunities to meet your prince. That is a duty both Antony and I share."

"But if he is my soul mate won't he enjoy the same things as me? Won't I find him in a place I enjoy spending time in?"

"Did you have any suggestions?"

She almost told him then and there about the library and Johann but the words didn't come out. She swallowed and said, "I found Adorjan to be a wonderful friend and companion. It's too bad he's not my princes as he's the only suitor I've met whom I genuinely like."

"I see."

"And every time I told you someone wasn't my prince you wouldn't listen. I want to find my prince, I'm not going to lie, and I'm not willing to believe Airon intends me to spend my life with someone who makes me nauseous."

"Antony is out of control, I agree. And he is being controlling, I've seen it. I have tried to hold his temper in check and stand up for you when I can, but he will not rest until your prince is found."

"I thought as much."

"For now focus on this investigation. My notes should keep you busy until you think of a way to deal with the guilds."

"You mentioned laws or regulations. You wouldn't happen to know them, would you?"

"I know they exist and I'm sure I could find them." He smiled. "My knowledge of the law is a tad rusty I'm afraid. That will keep my busy today. If I find something useful I will bring it to your attention."

"Thank you Master Salazar."

"I live to serve." He bowed to her and let himself out. *Yes, I will find the laws you need, archaic though they may be. And I will talk to*

Antony. I don't know when that man became so stubborn but he is not doing himself or Vonica any favours with the way he is acting.

After cancelling the private meetings between Vonica and her suitors Antony found representatives of the noble houses dogged his steps whenever he ventured out. He stopped going to the public wing of the temple complex except to supervise court and perform his stewards' duties. When that hadn't been enough he did his tasks from his study, sending orders or requests by messenger. It was tedious but it worked to keep the nobles away. For a time.

Soon he found them, or their messengers, strolling casually down hallways or through gardens where they might chance across him and beg a moment of his time. So he locked himself in his private suite. He had everything he needed to complete his work, except the odd book which he could send a servant to fetch for him, but he liked the study. It was roomier, more comfortable, and with better windows.

And my favourite chair right by the hearth. All I need to do is turn it just so to catch the afternoon sun in the summer. I wonder if Vonica would permit me to move that chair here? Would she notice if I switched the chairs?

The pounding at the door startled him. Servants knocked timidly. Lords and Ladies sent servants more often than coming themselves and when they did knock it was a politely demanding sound. Prim, precise. The sudden thought that it might be a guard come to report an emergency had him scrambling for the door.

Salazar stood in the hallway with his hands behind his back. His casual, patient, posture did not match the tone of his knocking. "Antony, we have much to discuss."

He stepped back, allowing his fellow steward into the room. "Come in, please, this doesn't sound like a conversation we should be having in the hallway. Is everything all right?"

"No."

"I see. Have a seat. Can I send for tea?"

"No, that won't be necessary."

"So, what is this about?"

"Did you receive a request from Princess Vonica?"

Antony snorted. "Did she bother you with one of those as well? I told her this was a bad idea."

"And I told her it was a good one. We won't agree, and that's fine, but you are sworn to serve her."

"I will not allow her to pursue this folly."

"She is pursuing it without you. You know what is required of you and you know the consequences for refusing."

"Come now, Salazar, no princess has ever dismissed a steward from his position in eleven rebirths."

"I shan't keep you, I know you're busy. I hope you will at least consider what I've said. Vonica was asking about laws and regulations that might be helpful to her dealings with the guilds and I'm sure she'll find that interesting as well. Oh, one last thing, are you familiar with Adorjan?"

"Adorjan Hearth-Glow? Yes. His uncle is Rheeya's steward; we had some classes together I think you'll recall. Alessandro. Why?"

"Oh, it seems he's been making quite the impression on the princess, at least in a professional capacity. His teachers sing his praises as well. The boy has a bright future, probably as soon as an appropriate position opens up. I'm quite busy as well so I'll go now. Good day." He left without dismissal or farewell. He stopped the first servant he passed and said, "I'll need to speak with the head of housekeeping immediately."

"Mrs. Bright? I believe she has the afternoon off today sir."

"Fetch her anyways. It is a special request and concerns the princess."

"Of course sir." The servant bowed and rushed off.

After long years of service, first as a maid, then training the new maids, and now as the head of housekeeping, Jenna Bright had earned the privileges of two half days off each week plus enough time to visit the temple for one weekly service and feast days. Her children were grown now, her girls all married and two of them expecting. They lived down in the city. One of her boys was a clerk at the merchant bank; the other had done the whole family beyond proud and become a guard. Her husband had been thrown from a horse a year ago and hadn't lingered long. She didn't much miss the busyness of parenthood but she did miss the quiet dependability and warm intimacy that had been hallmarks of her husband's personality.

She spent her free days folding her laundry and sipping tea by the fire with a good book. That is how the servant boy found her, though she looked to be dozing more than reading.

"I'm sorry Mrs. Bright. Master Sun-Wise wishes to see you right away."

She glared at the boy. "It is my rest time. Give him my apologies and tell him I will come after dinner."

"Of course, Ma'am. He did say it was urgent, though. And something to do with the Princess." He turned to deliver her reply.

"Wait. I'm coming. Master Sun-Wise isn't one to abuse his position and if it's for the princess I can at least come and hear him out."

Salazar let Mrs. Bright into his room and offered her a chair by the heart. "Not often I get the nice chair," she said. "Or any chair for that matter."

"This is not a usual request. In fact, I am going to ask you to bend one of your professional rules."

"Which rule would that be?"

"Discretion."

"Sir, the privacy of every person we serve is of utmost importance, especially that of the princess. For me to break that privacy, well, the situation would have to be exceptional."

"I understand. Let me explain the situation and what I would like you to do, and then you can tell me if it is possible."

The whispers started that evening in the kitchen with the cooks talking about the extra portions because the princess was entertaining over dinner again. The next morning maids were chatting on their way to the laundry about how wonderful it was that Vonica wasn't so lonely all the time. There were comments between errand boys that Vonica was keeping them all hopping. Wasn't it nice to see her passionate about something?

Somehow the conversations were always had within hearing of the staff who worked in the guest wings. They in turn whispered to the personal staff of the noble families. The word 'prince' was never uttered and yet every noble who heard the whispers leapt to the same conclusion. And they all clamoured to the same man for answers.

7th of Thornrise 24th Year of the 11th Rebirth
Sun-Song Estate, Sun Temple Province

Johann found his mother and his sister in the dining room. He glanced around. "Where's Father? And Tullius?"

"Business I'm afraid," Lady Francesca said. "They left not long ago. This business with the fire has everyone on edge."

"Yes. It's tragic. When is the service going to be?"

Francesca shrugged. "I haven't asked. I'm sure your father knows. Or Master Octavian. Come and eat."

It was a larger, fancier breakfast than he was accustomed to and when he thanked the servant who brought his plate his mother raised both eyebrows. Luckily she said nothing.

"How are your studies Ioanna?"

His sister's face lit up in a smile. "When Father said you were coming home I wanted to write you and ask you to bring some books for me but Father said the letter wouldn't reach you in time. I wish he would have told me sooner so I could have added a list to his letter. Of course, I don't even know if you can take books away from the capital. Can you?"

He was grinning like a fool but his sister was one of the few people he actually liked. She was perhaps the only thing about home he truly missed, though he tried to hide it when he spoke of home so he wouldn't grow melancholy. "Depends on the title. Some I could have borrowed a few I could have bought. What were you interested in?"

"I can't tell you now!"

"Why not?"

"What if it turns out you could have brought it? I don't want to know. It's too painful to think about."

"Okay, okay, but let me know if you change your mind."

"I won't."

"Have you considered visiting me in the Capital?"

Her entire demeanor shifted as though he'd slapped her and she stared at her plate.

"What?"

"Don't mention Ioanna studying in the capital in your father's hearing," Francesca said. "You missed that argument. It has already been decided. Ioanna will stay here. Your father is already looking for a suitable husband for her."

"Of course," Johann said. "Forgive me. I hadn't realized the question would cause a disturbance."

Later Johann went in search of his sister. She wasn't in the library, the study, or the yard, and she wasn't answering her door. He was certain anyone else would simply assume she was occupied somewhere with their mother, or had gone down to the village, or was simply refusing to answer her door. No one else had spent time with her, not even Tullius who was Father's shadow even as a boy. No one else would know about the old storage room behind the pantry or the dusty old furniture two misunderstood children had turned into their personal haven.

He waited until the servants were busy elsewhere and slipped through the old familiar door. There was a candle flickering on the side table so he knew he had found her even before he saw her.

Ioanna was curled up in a dusty old arm chair with a book on her lap. She looked up and smiled at him. "I wasn't sure you'd remember. You've been away so long."

"I've visited."

"You always visit Father. We never have time."

He settled on a low stool. "I know but I could never get a lot of time off from school."

"You're a scholar now. Will you stay longer this time, please?"

"What are you reading?"

"You're not answering me. That means it's an answer I won't like."

"I think you're the smartest person in this family."

She broke down crying. The book slid forgotten from her lap. Johann reached down and picked up the book, smoothing the bent page before closing it. He recognized the title. It was an impressive volume on theology.

He set it aside and reached for her hands. "What did I say?"

"Octavian told Father I wouldn't succeed in any further studies and that there was no point in sending me to the capital. Father even dismissed Master Erasmus."

"You're reading The Rise of the Holy Sun, and without your teacher here to help you with it. Does it make sense to you?"

"Some of it." She sniffled. "But I can't ask anyone to explain it."

"They have special dorms and classes for noble girls. And if Father is so set on you marrying you'd have the chance to meet many noble men. More than you're meeting now."

She shook her head. "It doesn't matter. Father won't listen to me, or you. He only listens to Octavian and his own whims."

"Do you think a royal summons would change his mind?"

She stared at him for a long moment. "You wouldn't dare fake a royal summons. Octavian would double check its authenticity. Father would disown you. The Library would expel you. You'd have a single name and no job!"

"I don't need to fake it. I just need to ask a favour."

"A favour? Johann, have you met the princess?"

He smiled.

"Tell me everything! What is she like?"

"All right, but you must keep it a secret. Tullius would be angry if he knew."

"I promise."

"I think she is a lot like you, Ioanna. She is sad a lot, and lonely. She loves books, especially books about adventures."

"Is it true about her scar?"

Johann nodded. "Sometimes she forgets about the scar and she forgets to be shy and sad, and then all you see is her smile and her passion and her strength. But she's so concerned that everyone is staring at her scar."

"Are they?"

"Yes, they are. But I don't know if she's self-conscious because they stare, of if they stare because she's self-conscious and that inadvertently calls attention to it."

"What happened to her?"

"I don't know exactly. No one talks about it and I don't ask."

"Aren't you curious?"

"Not really, no."

"How do you know so much about her?"

So Johann told her all about that first day Vonica joined him in the library and some of their more interesting afternoons and he soon had her smiling and laughing.

"You really fed the princess?"

He nodded.

"And she really ate it? I thought you said the food they give you in the scholar's wing wasn't the greatest."

"It's fine, just not fancy."

"But she ate it?"

"Yes."

"She seems nice. And so normal."

"We're not normal, Ioanna, at least the people in the village wouldn't think so."

"I forget, they let commoners attend school in the capital with the nobles."

"Commoners make good priests in small villages, among other things. I saw the way Mother looked at me at breakfast. There's a reason most low level scholars are not on the guest lists of any fancy dinner parties."

"I thought it was because you were all so boring," she said. There was a twinkle in her grey-blue eyes.

"Ha ha. Hey, I've been wondering, with me being so boring and all, why did Father call me home? He and Tullius have this emergency well in hand."

"I don't know. But I'm glad you're here."

Tullius and his father, Lord Yannakis Sun-Song, didn't return until dinner that evening. Johann was aware of a tension at the table that he hadn't noted before even though the news was mostly good. The first group of workers had arrived from the capital. Some of the carpenters brought news of a mine collapse in the mountains and a nasty dispute between the Stone Clan miners, led by a common-born overseer and the head of the Iron Guild in the Stone Clan province.

"This is what comes from promoting commoners. They have no idea what it takes to manage something as large and complex as a mine. And they're oblivious as to how to negotiate with nobles. If this dispute had been between two nobles it would have been settled already."

"I've met some talented and intelligent commoners," Johann said. "I had lunch with a priest who grew up the son of a poor village teacher. He knew more about the education system than any scholar I'd spoken to prior."

"Sure, sure, among our people perhaps, where we put a higher value on education, but other provinces don't have that focus. They don't have access to teachers and scholars the way we do."

"Yes they do. It's one of the services our people provide to support the pact."

Yannakis frowned and set his fork down. "And how many miners and pig farmers have you met in that fancy library of yours?"

"None," Johann muttered, feeling all of eight years old again.

"That's right."

"But how many have you met?" Johann persisted.

"We have commoners in the village," Tullius said.

"What are their names? How many children do they have? How long did they attend school? How many of them have you actually had contact with? There are few if any in the library but I've met others – gardeners, hawk masters, smiths …"

"I'm far too busy to sit around gossiping with farmers and hunters," Yannakis replied.

"Then how can you claim to know anything about them?"

"Octavian keeps me well informed. He has worked with commoners many times and has witnessed first-hand their incompetence."

"Wouldn't you rather know for yourself?"

"I pay Octavian to advise me because I don't have time to handle all my work plus all the research and study that always needs doing. Not all of us have the luxury of being able to spend all day lost in books and make believe." He picked up his fork again. "We begin rebuilding tomorrow. That mine collapse could make it difficult to get lumber though."

"We have time," Tullius said.

"They need homes if they're are to produce crops to see us through the winter. Johann, meet me in my study after dinner. I have something important I wish to discuss with you."

"Yes Father."

Johann sat in the straight-backed chair in front of his father's desk for over an hour. Finally the door behind him opened. He stood to greet his father but came face-to-face with Octavian. They were dressed very much alike except for the difference in sash.

"Your father is unable to meet with you this evening after all. Something important came up. He'll meet you tomorrow morning after breakfast."

Johann bit back his first reply which would not have been respectful and managed a, "Thank-you."

Octavian nodded.

"Tell me, did the new birds arrive for the eyrie?"

"Yes, they did. You wish to send a letter?"

"Yes. Just to keep Master Bright-Quill updated. I wasn't able to give them a firm date for my return when I left."

"You can give me the letter if you wish and I will see that it is sent."

"Thank-you but it gives me the chance to stretch my legs. Scholars spend so much time at a desk." Johann stood and stepped towards the door but Octavian didn't move.

"My other various duties as steward spare me from that particular occupational hazard. Very well. If you do require anything do not hesitate to ask."

"Thank-you." He stepped past the steward and returned to his room.

The letter he penned was not to Master Bright-Quill but to Princess Vonica.

Princess, my apologies for leaving on such short notice. My presence was requested at home. My father thanks you for sending aid in the wake of the fire. They will begin rebuilding tomorrow. The reason I am writing you is because of my sister, Ioanna.

I mean, I am also writing to let you know that I am all right and that I am missing our time together in the library. But my sister, I think you can help her. I think you would like her.

She is bright, reading books I wouldn't choose for pleasure and understanding at least part of it. I believe this is why she has never accompanied my parents to the Capital, strange as that sounds. Perhaps if you decide to go forward with the royal ball you could extend my sister a formal invitation? My father would not be able to refuse you.

I am concerned about things at home. Perhaps I have been away too long but things have changed here, and I don't just mean because of the fire. My father wishes to speak with me privately tomorrow. After that conversation I will have a better idea of how long I will be staying here.

If there are no hard feelings over my sudden and unannounced departure perhaps we could resume our library rendezvous upon my return. I would very much like that.

I know this will appear an odd request but do not reply to this letter. Until I know if there is something disconcerting happening here I cannot guarantee that a message would reach me unread by other eyes.

I hope you are keeping well. I truly do miss you. Your friend, Johann Sun-Song, Scholar.

Most Animal-People Johann met were lean muscle and long of limb. Ferrand Hounds, the hawk master at the Sun-Song estate was built more like the Stone Clan or Metalkin. He laughed about his size and told everyone, "Not all Animal-People look like deer, some of us look like bears!"

"Master Johann," he said with a voice that matched his large frame and wide smile. "It's been too long. What can I help you with?"

"A letter, if you will. Master Octavian said you had birds again."

"I did. Your father and his steward had many messages to send and now I only have one hawk remaining, at least until the others return with the replies. Is it an urgent message?"

"Not urgent, per say, but important. And not going far. Just to the Capital."

"Well, that's what they're here for. Headed for the city or the temple buildings?"

"The temple buildings." He handed over the letter.

"The princess?" Ferrand said, glancing down at the letter. "I hadn't expected that."

Johann just shrugged.

"Telling tales, Johann?"

Now Johann felt his cheeks heating up. He straightened, ready to defend himself with vague half-truths to protect the contents of that letter.

Before he could say anything Ferrand nodded. "Good. You'll be telling more before you leave here."

The door opened and Octavian stepped in. Ferrand acknowledged him with a nod. "And who are you sending this to?"

"Uh, Master Bright-Quill in the library of the temple complex," Johann said.

"Very good. I'll make sure that it gets to the right place. It is always good to see you, Master Johann."

"Thank-you Ferrand."

Johann returned to his room. Ferrand's reaction to the letter, and to Octavian's sudden presence, added to his list of concerns. *Why doesn't Ferrand trust Octavian?*

7th of Thornrise 24th Year of the 11th Rebirth
Sun Temple, Sun Temple Province

Vonica met Antony in the hallway and tried to ignore his critical stare. "Princess," he said. "I was just coming to fetch you for court. Surely you aren't planning to wear that."

She looked down at her dress. The fit and quality of craftsmanship were exquisite but the fabric was plain and heavy. She was wearing boots, not her usual soft shoes, and a pair of beautiful leather gloves. She looked back at Antony. "Yes, I am wearing this today. It's perfect for what I need to accomplish and I won't be hearing petitions today."

"You what?"

She tried to hide the way his harsh voice made her cringe. *This is easier with Salazar standing beside me. Or Adorjan.*

"There are people waiting with petitions."

She stood a little straighter. "They'll wait until tomorrow then. I have more important things to do." She started walking.

Antony dogged her steps. "And if one insists? Where can I expect to find you this morning?"

"I'm going into the city. I've already made the necessary arrangements with the captain of the guard. Now, if you'll excuse me, my escort should be waiting for me in the courtyard."

"Why don't I come along with you? It won't take long to saddle another horse."

"No!" She looked away. "I mean, that's not necessary. I'll have guards, and Adorjan has agreed to come with me to assist with my papers and such. I didn't want to trouble you. I know you're very busy with your own work."

"If you are not hearing petitions and will not be here to help with planning the ball I'm not sure there's much more for me to do until you return."

"Excellent. Then you'll have the information I requested yesterday ready for me at my return."

Her knees were shaking under her skirt. She had more conflict ahead of her today and she'd already had her fill of it. Fortunately he was too stunned to follow after her any further.

The day was bright and she tried to shake off her mood. Her escort was indeed waiting with ten saddled horses.

"Good morning Princess Vonica," said one of the guards. "My name is Cyril Bright. The Captain put me in charge of your escort today. We had a horse saddled for you as per your request but if you'd rather a carriage we can still arrange that."

"I'd rather ride today," Vonica said. She hadn't ridden outside of the corral in years but she thought the carriage would send the message that she was weak and pampered, easier to push aside, easier to ignore. She could not afford to be ignored today. Adorjan and Cyril gave her a leg up and soon they were riding down the wide road from the Temple Complex to the City. Her first stop was the Merchant Bank.

For all the wealth and power contained within the Merchant Bank was a plain building. The only outward sign of its great importance was its size. Even inside, while everything was of the finest craftsmanship and was cleaner than the royal wing of the Temple, the atmosphere was underwhelming. As a child she was disappointed.

Every clerk stopped what they were working on to stare at her as she and her escort walked past their desks. The man who scurried to meet them wore a plain linen robe with a red sash that was secured at his hip with an ornate gold buckle.

"Princess," he stammered. "This is a surprise. How may I help you? Or who can I fetch to help you?"

"No, don't disturb anyone. I understand the masters of the bank are busy dealing with the passing of your archivist."

"Yes, a sudden and tragic business. May I ask why you are here?"

"I am here to pick up records that I need. I've brought my own help. If you would escort us to the archive rooms we won't keep you from your work any longer than necessary."

"I'm sorry Princess; I cannot allow anyone into the archives alone."

"I won't be alone. I'll have my guards and my scholar."

"I mean, you need someone from the bank there with you."

"I am someone from the bank."

He just stared at her.

"As the princess of the Sun Temple Province I'm the head of the bank. That means these are my archives and I can access them any time I please. Please show me the way to the archives."

The little man nodded and hurried away. Vonica and Adorjan followed behind with the guards in tow. He led them to a heavy door at the end of a long hall. He opened the door for her and then took off.

"Nervous, isn't he?" Vonica said.

"And you're not?" Adorjan said.

She smiled thinly. "Was it obvious?"

"No."

"Hmm, no light inside. I guess no one has been down here since Master Heart-Flame's death." She turned to Cyril. "Grab that torch from the wall there. And be careful with it. I'd rather have a lantern but we need to get this done."

Adorjan went straight to work, examining the titles on the books on the table while Vonica searched the shelves.

"But I work here!"

Vonica and Adorjan looked at the door. "Keep looking," she said softly. She took a deep breath and went out to find the guards had halted an elderly man.

"It's all right. I don't think he means me harm."

"Mean you ..? Do you know who I am?"

Her lessons on important members of the important families had begun when she was very young and she'd met this man once before. Confidently she said, "Of course I do. You are Quinlan Golden-Heart, son of Barret Golden-Heart, and the head of the Merchant Bank. I was sorry to hear of Master Heart-Flame's passing."

"I mean no offense Princess but you shouldn't be here."

"The records I require are very important and I cannot wait for them."

"Princess, this is highly unusual. We don't allow people access to our records. Discretion demands only authorized members of the bank have access to these records."

"Master Golden-Heart, need I remind you that I am the head of the bank and therefore your boss?" Her heart was hammering away in her chest. She hoped her shaking hands weren't noticeable.

"An honorary title, nothing more. No princess has ever meddled in our affairs before. I am insulted by your presence here. I demand you leave at once."

Vonica had heard that tone many times before. As a child she and the other princesses had received numerous scoldings. Somehow the other three, even Taeya, had remained defiant in the face of these onslaughts. Vonica was always the first to give in and apologize, usually through tears. This reaction hadn't changed as she matured.

Each confrontation with Antony White-Cloud made her want to hide in her room, wrapped in a blanket.

You cannot give up now! You are the princess, the keeper of the pact, and that is more than an honorary title. You're doing nothing wrong. Don't let him intimidate you.

She still felt intimidated but she cleared her throat and said, "I need those records and I need them now. If you're not here to help you may return to whatever it was you were doing before coming down here." When he just stood and gaped at her she added, "I can have someone escort you if you like."

"I'm going. But I'm reporting this intrusion."

"Report it? To whom? I'm the Princess."

He spun around, his robe billowing around his ankles. When he was gone Vonica leaned back against the wall. Tears stung her eyes. "It had to be done," she whispered.

"Pardon me Princess?"

"No, nothing."

Adorjan appeared beside her. "Come double check I've got everything you need and then we'll move on before they can call the city guard on us."

"Imagine the scandal," she murmured. "The princess arrested as a thief."

From the bank they moved on to the Gold Guild. Vonica didn't have as much authority here so when the clerk asked her to wait for the guild master she had to wait. What she lacked in authority she made up for in influence and the guild master, a surprisingly young man with the jet black hair so common among the Metalkin, didn't keep her waiting long.

"Princess Vonica Bright-Rose, you honour me with your visit. I am Master Galen Forge-Strength."

"How long have you been the head of the Gold Guild in this province?"

"Nearly a year now. Don't let my youthful appearance fool you, Princess. I am fully capable of leading this guild."

"I have no doubt in your ability to keep this guild profitable. I do, however, wish to make sure your goals do not put my people at risk."

"Ah yes. As I said in my letter, if there is a report of abuse or wrong doing I would happily assist you in any way to see that justice is done. Our records are reviewed by the Merchant's Bank and by officers appointed by the guild's Grand Master. They have found no errors or cause for concern."

"I'm afraid you have no choice in the matter. This goes beyond Grand Masters." She handed him the scroll from Princess Mallory. The important passage was underlined. She waited while he read it.

His lips thinned to a line and he nodded. "I'll fetch them."

"Master Hearth-Glow will accompany you. He knows what I am looking for."

The Silver Guild was a repeat of the Gold Guild but Master Forge-Strength must have sent word ahead because after that they had problems or delays, not until they reached the Jeweller's Guild.

They sat at the guild hall for a full hour before someone came to speak with them. The guild master was thin and stooped his once dark hair now overwhelmingly white. He was leaning heavily on an ornate cane and moved with slow, shuffling steps. Vonica got up and helped him to a chair.

"Master Royal-Gold, when I saw a different name on the latest correspondence from the guild I had thought you had finally retired."

"Mostly, my dear. I have some good assistants helping me with the day-to-day tasks around the guild. I apologize for keeping you waiting. I was out of the building and it takes me some time to get anywhere. Now, what can I do for you my dear?"

"I need to review some of your guild records."

"Has there been a complaint?"

"Not exactly, not from my province."

"Then I'm not sure why you are here."

"Have you heard about what is happening in the Stone Clan territory?"

"No, I've heard nothing."

Vonica frowned. "Did you get my letter?"

"No. One of my assistants must have dealt with it."

"I have a letter here from Princess Mallory. Can you read it or would you like me to read it to you?"

"I can barely walk and I tire easily but my eyes still work just fine."

She smiled and handed him the letter. While Master Royal-Gold was reading she glanced at Adorjan. He was still as a statue, his face neutral. His eyes shifted in her direction and the corners of his mouth settled into a frown for a second before his face became blank again.

"If Princess Mallory believes a review is necessary then of course you will have the records you need. The bell there, ring it please." When a young clerk appeared in the doorway he said, "We will need access to the archives."

"Yes sir."

"Master Royal-Gold, my assistant knows what I need. You don't need to make the extra trip down. I'll stay here and keep you company."

"You're so considerate." He nodded to the clerk.

Adorjan followed the clerk down to a dust room nearly identical to the ones he'd been working in all day. *The bank and the guilds don't care for their archives the way the scholars do.*

The clerk lit the lantern inside the doorway. There was a ledger open on the table along with pens and ink. One of the shelves held another two volumes. The remainder of the shelves were empty, even of dust. Adorjan frowned. "Where are the rest of the records?"

"I don't know." The clerk shrank back. "I swear I don't know. They didn't tell me anything."

"Who?"

The clerk shook his head, his hands up as though he expected a blow.

Adorjan gathered the three volumes and returned to the princess. She was laughing when he marched in and dropped the books on the table.

"What's this?" Master Royal-Gold said. "I expected a scholar to have more care for books, even if they are ledgers."

"You found everything we needed so soon?" Vonica said.

"These are the only ledgers in the archives," Adorjan said.

"Nonsense," Master Royal-Gold said. He used his cane to pull himself to his feet. He wobbled and Vonica reached out to steady him. She hovered the whole way down the hall but he needed no further help. The clerk was waiting at the door, wringing his hands. Master Royal-Gold surveyed the empty room. "I will look into this matter. No one is supposed to remove or destroy records without permission. There is procedure for this."

"I leave this to you then, Master Royal-Gold. We have much to review. Hopefully you locate the missing archives soon."

"Both you and Princess Mallory will be informed as soon as I have any answers."

"My thanks. May your people's spirits give you strength and may Airon give you wisdom."

Vonica and Adorjan rejoined their escort outside. The packs on the horses were loaded with books and scrolls.

"You have a lot of work to do." Adorjan carefully added the three ledgers to the pack so he wouldn't have to look at Vonica.

She paused, poised to climb into the saddle. "Me? You mean you aren't going to help?"

"I wouldn't presume to be welcome on such an important task. Surely your stewards are better trained to handle such matters."

"I will need your help. You studied the Metalkin and their economic traditions. I'll need you insights on this."

"Then I would be honoured to help."

"Let's go then. *We* have a lot of reading to do."

After a late dinner Vonica returned to her room. She settled in her favourite chair and closed her eyes until she heard the rattle of a tea tray. Mary was pouring tea into Vonica's favourite cup and had tucked a sweetened nut roll on the tray.

"Thank-you Mary."

"Can I bring you anything? A blanket? A book?"

"Oh, no, please. No books," she groaned. "By the time we stopped for dinner the words were dancing on the page and it felt like someone had hit me on the forehead with a blacksmith's hammer."

"Then I'm afraid I have bad news M'Lady. A hawk arrived for you from Sun-Song estate." She set the scroll on the table. "I'll just lay out your bed things and turn the covers down before I go." She went across the room working so quietly it was easy for Vonica to forget that she was there.

For a long time she sat sipping hot tea. She didn't even notice when Mary went out. Finally curiosity got the better of her and she picked up the scroll. The signature was the first thing revealed and she was pleasantly surprised to see Johann's name there. She unrolled to the beginning and began reading, her tea and her headache forgotten. She read quickly and, though the letter was curious, by the end she was smiling.

8th of Thornrise 24th Year of the 11th Rebirth
Sun-Song Estate, Sun Temple Province

After breakfast Johann reported to his father's study where Yannakis was signing papers under Octavian's watchful eye. He sat down across from his father. "Good morning, Father, Master Octavian. I hope you didn't have an urgent message to send last night. Ferrand mentioned he only had one bird ready to leave."

"Who were you writing to?" Yannakis said, not looking up.

"Master Bright-Quill."

His father nodded and continued reading.

"You needn't be concerned," Octavian said. "I went to the eyrie to check for replies. There were none, of course. Not surprising. Some were letters whose replies could not be rushed, others were sent to men who will not be rushed. I hope you receive a more timely reply."

Yannakis handed Octavian the stack of signed papers. "If that is all?"

"Yes sir."

"Leave us then. I must speak with my son."

"Of course, sir." He bowed slightly and left.

Johann couldn't help my wonder if Octavian was hovering in the hallway attempting to listen in through the heavy wooden door.

"I understand your work is going well and you are making a name for yourself at the library."

"Yes Father."

"So you know a great many scholars and priests?"

"I've met a lot of people, yes."

"Have you taken the opportunity to visit with the higher ranking priests?"

"There's not much social contact between the scholars and the priests. I had some classes with some of the acolytes years ago but for the most part we live and work at different ends of the temple complex."

"And the noble families at court?"

"I don't often attend court functions."

"So you spend all your time studying in the library?"

"No. I spend all my time completing my work for the scholars. I have illuminated some prominent manuscripts and my work is often sought out by the most important scholars."

"But you work alone and do not socialize?"

"Most of the time, yes. Why all the interest in how I choose to spend my time and who I choose to spend it with? I have done nothing to sully the family name."

"And nothing to help it, it appears. I had hoped you would have made some friends that would be useful to us."

If only you knew. "Sorry to disappoint you. Was there anything else?"

"Yes. Your brother will be attending the royal ball. You need to be ready for the strong possibility that Tullius is the princess's soul mate."

"Oh?"

"When your mother was pregnant with your brother there were rumours. The princess was ill, the prince had recently returned to the sun. Everyone was rushing to conceive. Then, you were born less than a year after your brother. When you were born a boy the priests saw it as a sign that Airon had claimed Tullius and had given us you to replace him as my heir."

"So why did you allow me to go to the Capital? Why not send Tullius?"

"The scholars were never interested in Tullius, and you were not interested in staying here. I had hoped you would make important friends while in the Capital. It quickly became apparent you were in love with those damn books. If I could have pulled you out of your classes without raising suspicions …" He sighed. "I don't think it would have helped. You would have run back the first chance you got. And we are so far down the political ladder right now I knew your brother, and you, would be near the end of the list."

"So if I was such a failure at making connections why didn't you send Ioanna to court? She's more social than I am."

"If Tullius is the prince he'll never have any children and you've proven yourself to be hopeless when it comes to marriage. I don't want to see my line end."

"What does that have to do with where Ioanna studies?"

"I can see it in her eyes. If she sets foot in that damned library she'll never want to come home. I'll never be able to secure her a proper marriage."

"She'll meet more people in the capital."

"Like you did? Pah. No. Better off keeping her here. Besides, I've already had an offer for her hand. She's shown no interest in him so far and I haven't mentioned it to her yet, but it's an ideal match."

"Who is he?"

"Octavian Gold-Hearth."

"He's older than I am!"

"He's noble born, educated, and loyal to our family. He's knows her and has always been kind to her. I have no reason suspect he would be unkind to her. That's all a father can hope for when finding a match for his daughter, isn't it?"

"Of course. Do you have a bride for me hiding around a corner somewhere?"

"No, of course not. I had hoped you'd come home with good news in that area."

"Why did you call me home now? Why not wait until after the royal ball?"

"Because there's no point in you attending the ball."

"What?"

"You are needed here. I know you've studied history and politics and mathematics but now you need to learn how to apply those things to ruling an estate and a village."

"Tullius is your eldest son and your heir. Won't he be angry that you're preparing me to take his place?"

"Airon himself wants you to do this. There is no arguing with the gods."

And no reasoning with you it seems. Still, the Capital is less than a day's hard ride from here. I can slip out just before dawn and be eating dinner with the scholars tomorrow night. I can deal with father for a day. "All right. I have no other plans. Do you want to begin now?"

Yannakis' eyes narrowed. "Just like that?"

"I don't know if Tullius is the prince or not but you are right, it doesn't hurt to be prepared. You granted me all these years to study. It's time to repay that kindness and do my part for the family."

"Good, that's good to hear."

"I do need to write Master Bright-Quill. I am part way through a job for him. He'll have to send everything here so I can complete it in my spare time."

"You said you were ready to put aside this foolish endeavor."

"I've undertaken a contract, Father. I must complete it or it will reflect poorly on my professionalism and my family."

"Be quick about it then. I want to get to the village this morning and you should come with me."

"I will write my letter, change my clothes, and meet you at the stables."

He changed clothes first to give himself time to get his thoughts in order. When he sat down to write he found his hand was trembling.

He delivered the letter to Ferrand and headed for the stables. *And now to play the devoted son.*

8th of Thornrise 24th Year of the 11th Rebirth
Sun Temple, Sun Temple Province

With renewed energy Vonica started on the record books right after breakfast. So far they had only managed to sort through the books and select those that looked most promising. Today the studying began in earnest.

Since Rheeya's problems were with the Iron Guild Vonica began there. Adorjan soon joined her, taking up a book form the Gold Guild as it was closest at hand. "What are we looking for again?"

"I don't know," Vonica confessed. "Something odd, something not right."

They settled in to their task working silently side-by-side. That is where Mary found them near midday.

"M'Lady, a message for you."

"Thank-you."

"Will you be taking your meal here?"

"No, I think a rest is in order. Have them prepare a meal for two and come fetch me when it is ready."

"Yes, M'Lady."

"The princess honours me," Adorjan said. He hadn't looked up from the ledger he was skimming through.

She gave Adorjan a wry look, which he completely missed. "Can we please stop with the honours and the formalities?"

"You're my princess."

"I'd like to count you among my friends. I have so few friends."

"You know, Princess, you are bright, fun to talk to, and you have a surprising sense of humour. I'm certain that if you invited some of the young women from the noble families to join you at court as your predecessors did you would quickly find many friends."

"No. No I will not."

"Princess …"

"No, you weren't here. You didn't see. When Rheeya and Betha and Taeya left they tried. They invited all these eleven and twelve and thirteen year old girls to live here and attend classes with me. There were some boys too but we didn't see them often. It was horrible! After a few months they sent them all home."

"What happened?"

"I wanted to hear all about their homes. Some were living in other provinces. I wanted friends to play with as I did with the other princesses. All they did was giggle and gossip and usually they giggled at me."

"Because of your scar?"

"Because of my scar. Because I was clumsy. Because I was shy. Because when I blush my scar is even more noticeable. Because they liked to laugh at me when I ran away crying from their teasing."

"Not everyone is like that," Adorjan said.

She wiped the tears away with the back of her hand. "You're not, but every other suitor has been just like that."

"Your prince won't be."

"Perhaps you are my prince after all."

"No. I really don't think so. But I would be honoured to be counted among your friends, Vonica."

"Thank-you."

"What news?"

"Hmm? Oh, the letter." She opened it and found a short, hurriedly scrawled note from Johann. Her heart leapt. *He's coming back tomorrow!* Then she frowned. *What is going on there?*

"Vonica, is everything all right?"

"I don't know, but I'll find out tomorrow. Master Johann is returning tomorrow and he has urgent news he cannot disclose in a letter."

"More trouble? Airon guide us."

There was a knock at the door. "M'Lady? The meal is ready."

"Thank-you Mary. I need a break from all this work."

9th of Thornrise 24th Year of the 11th Rebirth
Sun-Song Estate, Sun Temple Province

Johann had barely slept. By candlelight he stuffed his clothes back in his travel bag. He'd already made arrangements with the stable master and planned to pay the man well if he came through. *No matter. I'll walk back if I must.*

He blew out the candle and slipped through the still quiet corridors. Not even the servants were stirring yet. The guard at the door nodded as he approached.

"Master Johann, you're up early this morning."

"Just feeling restless. I thought some fresh air would do me good."

"And your bag?"

"Just some light reading. I'll ride up the bluff to that sheltered spot."

The guard was eyeing the bag which was round and lumpy, not flat and angular. Johann handed him a few coins.

"You will tell my father I've gone up to the bluff when he asks, won't you?"

"Yes sir, always happy to help."

His horse was waiting for him. She seemed half asleep, a sharp contrast to the urgency that kept Johann's heart pounding.

"Master Johann, your horse, as promised." Master Clyde handed over the reins.

Johann handed over a small purse. "Thank-you for this. You'll tell my father I've gone out to the sheltered place at the top of the rise for me?"

"Certainly. It's always my pleasure to help."

"I know. And thank-you."

"Master Johann?"

"Yes?"

"Ride fast. Your father is an early riser and an unforgiving man."

Johann nodded once, secured his bag, and swung into the saddle. By the time the sun had cast pink light over the bottoms of the clouds the estate was out of sight behind him.

9th of Thornrise 24th Year of the 11th Rebirth
Sun Temple, Sun Temple Province

"I'm sorry, she's dining."

The guard's words cut into the conversation and Vonica and Adorjan both stopped laughing. He raised his eyebrows.

"I don't know," she answered.

"I'll look." He went to the door and opened it to find a man in travel clothes pleading with the guard in the hallway.

"She's expecting me, just ask."

"Master Sun-Song?" Adorjan said.

The man looked up. "Yes."

"You're early. Have you eaten?"

"No. Who are you?"

"Master Hearth-Glow. Please, join us; we'll have another place brought up." Adorjan stepped back and let Johann into the cozy dining room.

Vonica looked up and a smile blossomed on her face. "Johann!"

He couldn't help but return the smile, even if Master Hearth-Glow's presence here was a punch in his gut. "Vonica, it's good to see you again. I'm sorry for my sudden departure and for missing so many afternoons in the library."

"I haven't had time to visit the library since you left."

Another punch in the gut.

"I sent for you when I got the letter from Mallory but you had already left. But there's time for that later, tell me of home. How bad was the fire? Did the workers arrive?"

While they'd been talking Adorjan had been addressing the servants and now Johann sat in front of a clean plate while a servant filled his glass. Adorjan returned to his seat.

"Hasn't my father or his steward written you with updates?"

"Perhaps," Vonica said. "I've been busy."

"But you've gotten my messages?"

"Of course. The hawk master who sent them marked them urgent and personal so they were brought straight to me instead of being left on my desk. Of course sometimes correspondence from the estates goes to my stewards to handle. I haven't had time to check with them."

"No time for the library, no time for the mail, what have you been doing?" He refused to look at Master Hearth-Glow.

"Investigating the Metalkin guilds and the Merchant Bank."

"What? Are you insane?"

She flinched. "It's necessary."

"I don't doubt that for a minute. It's also startling. What happened? Who complained?"

"No one complained exactly," Vonica said.

"Vonica is acting at the suggestion of the Princess Mallory." Adorjan said.

Johann bristled. *And now he's calling her by her first name. Just who does he think he is?* He filled his plate and focused on eating for a moment.

"We've lots of work to do," Vonica said. "We could use some help."

He didn't respond.

She reached out and laid her hand on his wrist. "You will help, won't you?"

Was it the need in her voice or the touch? He didn't know for sure which but it made him look up into her eyes. Even her eyes, big and dark, were pleading with him. "Yes, of course. I'll need to speak with Master Bright-Quill. He's expecting me to return to work on that book."

"I'll speak to him and impress upon him the importance of our work here."

"Thank-you, that will help a lot."

"It's the least I can do. Now tell me about the fire."

"It started at the black smith's forge," Johann said.

"Excuse me," Adorjan said, standing suddenly. "I've just remembered something. I'll be right back."

"Hearth-Glow," Johann said after Adorjan had left. "Is this the suitor from the day you were late?"

"Yes."

"Have you two been spending much time together?"

"Just the last few days. His area of study makes him important to this investigation."

Adorjan reappeared with a large book open in his hands. He had a satchel slung over his shoulder and Johann could see it contained a second book. "Here, take a look at this." He pushed his plate aside and set the book down.

Vonica got up and stood beside him. "Which guild is this?"

"Iron."

Johann had no choice but to join them if he wanted to stay involved in the conversation. It would have been shorter to go left but that would have put Adorjan between him and Vonica so he went the long way around the table. The book was filled with neat columns of numbers and brief chunks of text. "You have the Iron Guild's ledgers?"

"All the guilds actually," Adorjan said.

"I'm impressed. So what exactly are we looking at?"

"Here," Adorjan pointed.

The text beneath his fingers read: 70 gold suns requested by village black smith, for forge repairs. Request received and settled.

In the next column was a red 40, then an account number and a black 40.

"So whoever asked for this forge asked for money to do repairs and got a smaller sum. What does that have to do with the forge at the Sun-Song Estate?" Johann said.

"I've noted a few places in all the guild records where some requests were underfunded and others were denied. I assumed each guild has a review board that evaluates each request and decides upon the necessity of the request. But Master Sun-Song's words made me suspicious. Look at the date on this specific request."

"That's only five weeks before the fire. Whose account is this?"

In response to Vonica's question he pulled out the second book. "Let's find out."

It took some flipping back and forth to find the correct entry. The account belonged to Cade Iron at the Sun-Song Estate.

"Five weeks before a fire destroyed this forge and half a village the Iron Guild refused to fully fund a repair request," Johann said.

"You said you noticed similar entries elsewhere?" Vonica said.

Adorjan nodded. "I'm afraid so."

"How many other forges are improperly maintained?" Johann said. "Do these ledgers hold records of other fires? Smaller fires that were never brought to Vonica's attention?"

"I can check," Adorjan said. "But the estate stewards might have records that would help us find those entries faster."

"I will write them," Vonica said. "Johann, will you write your father? There are some details I will need from him."

"That may not be wise. I didn't tell him I was leaving and he will not be pleased that I left."

"You'd best finish your story." She returned to her seat so Johann did the same.

He decided to start with what he was most sure of. "My father is anxious for me to marry. He seems to think my being in the capital is a waste of time. He will not send my sister to the capital and has a marriage in mind for her. She won't be happy with him and I'm sympathetic to her but there's nothing I can do. As far as my sister is concerned he's broken no laws and I have no reason to suspect the man he's chosen would hurt her physically."

"Still, you want me to issue her an invitation to the Capital?"

"Even if it's just so she has the chance to see it once before she is married."

"The man your father has in mind, he is twice named?"

"Yes."

"I'm sure he'll bring her to the capital. All nobles come once every few years for Holy Week at least."

Johann nodded.

"Is that all?"

"No. My father wanted me to stay at the estate and learn from him so I could inherit the estate and the village."

"Don't you have an older brother?"

"Yes."

"Isn't he supposed to inherit the estate?"

"Yes. But my father is convinced that Airon chose my brother as your prince."

"Do you believe that?"

"No."

Adorjan had only been half listening, most of his attention still on the ledger, but the absolute assertion of that one word made him look up. He watched the rest of their exchange with intense interest.

"Why not?" Vonica said.

Johann's cheeks darkened. "He doesn't like books and he doesn't thank servants. He's an insensitive braggart and you deserve better."

Adorjan cleared his throat. "I should go."

"Oh!" Vonica turned. "Please, let's finish dinner. I've let business interrupt."

"I didn't mean this second," Adorjan said. "I meant I should go to the Sun-Song Estate."

"What would you do there?" Johann said.

"Princess Vonica will send me to the Sun-Song estate because of her deep and honest concern for her people. She can't leave the Capital but she wanted to be more involved. I will be there to help in any way I can, and Vonica will give me some minor and temporary power to make decisions on her behalf in order to speed up the rebuilding process."

"You've got this all planned out it seems," Johann said. He took some more salad.

"Actually, I'm making it up as I talk." He put the books in the satchel and pulled his plate close again. "It's your family I'd be dealing with. What do you think? Would it work?"

"What would you really be doing?"

"Investigating the fire and sending daily reports back to the princess, maybe I could learn something useful."

"Be careful of Master Gold-Hearth. He was very interested in the letters I was sending to the Capital."

"Perhaps tomorrow morning while the princess takes care of her courtly duties you could tell me what you know of everyone I will have contact with."

"If Vonica agrees to send you. I could spare the time, yes." Spending time alone with this man was the last thing Johann wanted to do, but he couldn't refuse something that would help Vonica.

They both turned to Vonica. She was staring intently at the platter of pork. Her fingers drummed on the table next to her plate. Finally she said, "I think this is the right thing to do, yes, I'm almost certain it is. Yes. Adorjan I'll write a letter to Lord Sun-Song tomorrow and you can leave the morning after. Will that give you enough time to prepare?"

"I think so, yes."

"Write him a letter of introduction as well," Johann said. "It needs to have your signature and seal and list all of the permissions and privileges you grant Master Hearth-Glow. It must be formal and official and he will have to present it to my father upon his arrival."

Vonica nodded. "All right, I will, now, let's finish eating, please."

10th of Thornrise 24th Year of the 11th Rebirth
Sun Temple, Sun Temple Province

Johann flipped idly through one of the massive ledgers as he waited in the study. He'd skipped breakfast to be here this early but then he wasn't hungry either. He'd been stopped by a guard at the entrance to the royal wing and had expected another fight but the guard let him through as soon as he mentioned his name, as had the guard posted at the study door. When the door opened Johann glanced up. It was Adorjan, as he had hoped.

The other scholar smiled. "Master Sun-Song, I'll be happy for your help today. I have a lot of questions before I leave."

Johann hadn't expected anger to grip his chest so tightly or so suddenly. He took a deep breath. "Ask."

"Your father's steward, what was his name?"

"Octavian Gold-Hearth."

"Ah, an important family. They have a great many members working at the Merchant's Bank if I recall correctly. You said something about suspicious behaviour?"

"Expect him to watch you closely and resent your presence."

"I'm growing accustomed to people resenting my presence. That's one of the reasons I thought it beneficial I undertake this journey. I'm afraid word has spread of my assistance to the princess these past few days and some of her suitors are getting the wrong impression."

"What impression would that be?"

"That I'm her prince. Ridiculous but there is not convincing them that I'm not using this crisis to woo her. When I do eat in the scholar's wing I now dine alone or with common-born scholars. My father asks me every day if Vonica has chosen me yet. They cannot understand that I'm not her prince and have no interest in pretending that I am. It is frustrating and I welcome this break."

"I'm sure Vonica has enjoyed being around her if you are this open with her."

"I told her at our first meeting that I was not her prince. She was startled by that."

"Because she has feelings for you?"

"No, because she wasn't used to honesty from her suitors."

Johann felt the fist loosen its grip on his chest. "What else do you need to know?"

"Who is the black smith? Do you know anything about the healers? Who might help me and who I should be wary of?"

They spent the rest of the morning deep in conversation.

11th of Thornrise 24th Year of the 11th Rebirth
Sun Temple, Sun Temple Province

"I cannot stay," Vonica said. "My stewards insist I attend court again today. But you'll need this." She handed Adorjan a letter with a royal seal. "Present this to Lord Sun-Song and report to me daily."

"Of course I will. And you'll write if you have any questions about the ledgers?"

"I have Johann to help, but yes, I will."

"Then I am off."

"I envy you."

"I am certain you will see Sun-Song Estate very soon."

"How can you possibly know that?"

Adorjan shrugged. "I guess I don't. I hope you find what you are looking for."

"With your help I will. Good luck on the road."

He bowed and clambered onto his horse. Still wishing she could accompany him and see a little more of the world she watched him ride away. When he was gone through the gates she hurried back inside before Master White-Cloud could come looking for her.

11th of Thornrise 24th Year of the 11th Rebirth
Sun-Song Estate, Sun Temple Province

Adorjan could see the path of destruction the fire had taken as he rode through the village. Commoners with stained clothes and dirty faces watched him as he rode past. Everyone seemed busy cleaning away burnt rubble. The road curved left past the remains of a forge. Ahead in a field were several large tents and cooking fires. He continued up the rise to the walled estate.

The man tending the gate held a spear and wore an ill-fitted leather helmet but no other armor. Adorjan reined in his horse and looked down at the man. "Ho there, were is the regular guard?"

"Dinner sir. I'm just to mind the gate until he returns."

"I'm here to see Lord Sun-Song. It's important business."

"Go on in. One of the other boys at the stable will tend to your horse and point you in the right direction."

"Thank-you."

The courtyard was quiet. Adorjan swung down from his horse and led it to what remained of the stable. "Hello?"

A boy of twelve or fourteen appeared. "Yes sir?"

"See to my horse, boy. I hope to stay the night."

"Yes sir."

"I was told you could point me in the direction of Lord Sun-Song."

"Aside from telling you to go in the main door I don't think I'd be much help. But they can help."

Adorjan's gaze followed the direction of the boy's outstretched finger. Two guards were walking across the courtyard. For a moment he just watched t hem. They were lightly armored and carried swords. For the most part their job consisted of watching for thieves and Dark Spirits. Adorjan was neither and yet he hung back. He curled and stretched his fingers and focused on keeping his breathing steady.

"Your bags sir."

"Yes. Thank-you." With bags in hand he had no further reason to delay. He hurried to catch the guards. "Excuse me; I need to see Lord Sun-Song."

"It's dinner hour," said the smaller guard. "There's an inn in the village."

"It burned down," the larger man said.

"Right. You'll have to stay in the tents with the labourers. Come back in the morning."

"This is important," Adorjan said. He pulled the letter from his bag.

"I can take your message to Lord Sun-Song," said the smaller guard.

"Donatello, I have to get back to the gate. I can't just leave the boy there all night."

"Go on then, I'll deal with this."

"I don't need to be dealt with and I don't need you to take my message to Lord Sun-Song on my behalf. I am Adorjan Hearth-Glow, the nephew of Princess Rheeya Stone-Rose's steward and I have been personally selected by Princess Vonica Bright-Rose to deal with a situation here on her behalf. I need you to take me directly to Lord Sun-Song, now."

Donatello stood a little straighter. "Yes sir. Follow me."

Adorjan had grown up in the Capital. They had a small walled yard behind the house with a garden and stone benches in the shade.

There was no front yard or courtyard, just a gate that was watched by two men at all times and a wrought iron fence. Everything in the house was wood and brick with fine carpets and tapestries and paintings and windows everywhere. This estate was all stone, heavy and oppressive, or maybe that was the lack of windows. There were torches every few feet down the corridor but it wasn't the same.

Donatello opened a large door and led the way into a large dining hall. There were only two people, both women, sitting at the table. Donatello bowed. "Lady Sun-Song, an important visitor from the Capital to see you."

"Thank-you."

When Lady Sun-Song stood Adorjan could see the resemblance to Johann. She certainly had a narrower face, especially in the chin, but she had the same thick dark brown hair and the same dark eyes. When she moved he saw an easy grace and she greeted him with a warm smile. "Welcome friend. I am Lady Francesca." She offered her hand and he pressed his lips to the back.

"I am Adorjan Hearth-Glow."

"And this is my daughter, Ioanna."

He bowed as he turned to Johann's sister, still seated at the table. "Greetings." He looked up and the breath caught in his throat. Unlike Johann, Ioanna was fair-haired. She was smiling shyly, her hands in her lap.

This is what it's supposed to feel like. Does she feel it too? How could anyone fail to notice this? She has grabbed my heart, my very soul, without lifting a single one of her perfect fingers.

Adorjan cleared his throat. "Forgive my intrusion during dinner. I hoped to speak with your husband as soon as possible."

"Have you had dinner? If you've come from the Capital you've spent all day riding. Join us, please. There's plenty. And after you've eaten we'll see about finding you a room."

A master of misdirection under the guise of kindness. That's how Johann described her and I can see why. He'd promised himself he would not fall into her trap, that he would remain polite but focused on the task at hand. But that promise meant nothing now that he had met Ioanna. He smiled. "I would love to join you, thank-you." He chose the empty seat next to his hostess, across from Ioanna. "Your husband is not dining with you this evening?"

"He was called away by some important business. I'm afraid so many things need his attention, especially with the fire."

"Yes, tragic business that. I saw some of the damage on my way in. When will they begin rebuilding?"

"Already the eyrie and stables are under way. The town is taking longer. There is so much clean up to be done before building can begin."

"Understandable." A servant came with a fresh plate and Adorjan murmured "Thank-you."

Ioanna looked up, her eyebrows raised, but said nothing.

What was it Johann said about her? 'She could be your strongest ally, she was mine. She's the only one you can tell about the investigation.' Yes, an ally and hopefully much more.

"Since my business will have to wait, why don't you tell me all about your lovely home?"

Francesca preened at the compliment and the opportunity. "The estate has such a rich history."

With very little prompting Adorjan kept Francesca talking through the entire meal. When everyone's plate was empty she said, "You must be tired."

"The food and conversation were very refreshing."

"Well, at least the chance to wash up. Ioanna, would you show our guest to his room? East wing, second floor, there should be a bed made up."

"Of course." She dropped her napkin on her plate. "You had bags, correct? I'll have a servant bring them."

"No. It's okay. I prefer to carry my own bags." *I don't want a servant tagging along. I'd much rather the chance to speak with you in private.*

"Then follow me please. Good-night, Mother."

"You're not turning in so early again, are you?"

"I'm sorry. I still feel unwell and it leaves me so tired."

"All right. Master Adorjan, ring if you need anything. I'll send someone up shortly with a basin."

"You're very kind." He picked up his bags just inside the door and followed Ioanna out. "I'm sorry to hear you are not well," he said when they were alone.

"I'm fine," she said. "I just prefer time to myself and it seems lately my parents are reluctant to give it to me. This way they do not disturb me."

"How do you know you can trust me? I might tell your mother."

"I don't know, I just do. Are you going to tell my mother?"

"No."

"Then I suppose I'm a good judge of character. It's up the stairs here."

"Can I tell you a secret then? An exchange of trust?"

"Yes, you can trust me."

"I'm here to conduct an investigation into the cause of the fire, but your father mustn't know. He must think I've been sent here to help him or I will learn nothing."

"You are correct in that regard." She fell silent as she mulled his words over. "Here, this is your room."

"Thank-you."

"Will you let me help you?"

"I'm hoping you will."

"You're right, there is something going on. I wish I could tell you more but no one tells me anything important."

"Why not?"

"Because all I'm good for is securing some alliance or business deal through marriage. And who would want an educated wife?"

"I would." He cleared his throat. "That is to say, I know a lot of people who would."

"Thank-you. Whatever is going on here, my father is involved, and so is Master Gold-Hearth, the estate's steward. My brother likely knows something but I doubt he's pulling any strings or making any decisions."

"What about your other brother?"

"No, he's not involved. I'm certain of it."

"As am I, since he helped me prepare for this investigation."

"You know Johann?"

He nodded. "I met with him for some time yesterday."

A servant carrying a basin of warm water appeared at the top of the stairs.

"Good-night, Master Hearth-Glow."

"Good-night. I hope you are feeling better soon."

12th of Thornrise 24th Year of the 11th Rebirth
Sun Temple, Sun Temple Province

It was a lovely day, one of the first in a long time where the sun was not blocked by clouds. Court was completed early so Vonica decided to take a walk in the main garden before joining Johann in the library. Working in the study had been productive, and Adorjan's presence was not at all distressing, but it was good to be back in the library with Johann, even if it meant hauling books back and forth. She wandered the garden paths humming to herself. She had serious work ahead of her and yet she felt lighter than she had in days.

She paused at the gazebo to examine the roses. She knew nothing about roses or their growing season but she was happy to see they had buds interspersed between the leaves. *Soon. Soon there will be roses and it will be summer. I love to come here in the summer and sit on the bench in the shade surrounded by the scent of roses and read my books. Will he join me?* The image came suddenly to mind, vivid though unbidden, of lying on the bench, book in hand, head cushioned on the leg of another. Her prince. Was it possible? Was it that easy?

She was amazed by the sudden possibility and hurried down the path back towards the palace. Her route, shorter this time, took her down a different set of paths. She rounded a corner and found an artist seated on a folding stool with a canvas before him. There was something oddly familiar about him. She watched as he worked though she could only see the edges of the canvas.

He shifted in his seat revealing more of the painting. A border of roses so lifelike she could almost smell them, red hair, familiar eyes staring back at her, eyes she saw in every mirror and every darkened window. She'd seen dozens of portraits of herself and her predecessors but none that looked so ready to blink at any second. The detail was stunning and it drew her closer.

That's when she heard the humming. She couldn't name the tune but she'd heard it before. Sometimes in the library Johann would hum while he worked, quietly so it didn't disturb the other scholars, and it always made Vonica smile. Now it made her shake.

"No," she whispered.

He turned. And it was Johann. He was smiling but it turned to a look of concern. "Vonica? My Lady, what's wrong?"

"No," she said again, backing away, shaking her head.

"Princess?" He took a step towards her. She turned and fled.

It was Mary who found Vonica in her bed sobbing into her pillow. She hurried to the bed and sat beside her. "There now, Princess," she said, rubbing her back. "What's wrong dear?"

For a long time Vonica could only cry while Mary patted her back and murmured soothing words.

Twice when she was only a child she had cried hard into her pillow like this. Once had been the day Rheeya, Betha, and Taeya had left. They were all around twelve years of age and for the first time in her young life Vonica had felt completely alone. The other time she'd been even younger. The healer had done all she could. But for a child, seeing her face scarred like that, being told it was forever and being old enough to know what that meant, it wasn't enough. It still wasn't enough.

"Is there something I can do? Someone I can fetch for you?"

"Can you erase these scars?"

"Oh hush, is that why you're sobbing? I haven't seen you cry over that in years. Come on now, deep breaths, there's a good girl. Sit up now and I'll fetch the basin so you can wash your face."

"I always wished I could wash it away."

"You're being silly."

"I am not! I'm ugly. When everyone stares at the other princesses it's because they're beautiful and regal. They stare at me because I'm clumsy and ugly."

"You're no such thing."

Vonica sat up. "No? Do you know how I came to be scarred?"

"I was not working in the palace at the time, so no, I never did hear the whole story. We were told there was an accident. None of us are allowed to ask."

"An accident. Yes, well, I didn't do it on purpose so that much is true, but it was my own fault."

"You were a child, how ..?"

"We were running, the four of us. I can see them clear as day, the memory is so vivid. I dream it sometimes. Taeya and Betha out in front, as always. Taeya fleet footed and faster than any deer, Betha as graceful as a vine. Rheeya was sure-footed and fearless. She could have kept up with the other two but she held back so I wouldn't be left completely behind. She was kind like that. And I was clumsy and slow."

"Heard tell your predecessor was the last of her generation to pass on."

"So?"

"So, stands to reason then, that you're actually younger than the others by a few months at least."

"They didn't treat me as younger, they treated me as slow and clumsy and stupid. Only Rheeya treated me as a sister, truly. Still, they were all ahead of me when it happened. We turned a corner but I went wider than they did. Ran right into a candle stand. Oh, the clatter as iron hit stone. The candles fell free and some fell on me.

And that's how our province wound up cursed with a scarred princess."

"You truly believe all that? About being ugly and a curse?"

"It's not hard to believe when it's true. I'll take my midday meal here. And have all the ledgers brought here, they're in the study. I'll be working alone for the next few days. No interruptions."

"Of course, Princess."

13th of Thornrise 24th Year of the 11th Rebirth
Sun-Song Estate, Sun Temple Province

Lord Sun-Song had remained unavailable all that first evening. The next morning Adorjan had introduced himself and presented the letter from Vonica. Before Yannakis Sun-Song could really provide any information, or even really reply, Master Gold-Hearth came in with an emergency.

"If this is to do with the fire, perhaps I can help," Adorjan said. "After all, that's why I was sent."

"No," Master Gold-Heart said. "This is something else entirely."

Adorjan hadn't seen either of them for the rest of the day. He should have been upset since it was making his investigation difficult but he wasn't. It was simply too enjoyable to spend the time with Ioanna in the small keep library.

"You didn't have a library in your home?"

Adorjan shook his head. "We had shelves in the study and the sitting room, but the Temple Library was five minutes away. Anything we needed was there."

"You're so lucky. We had some very good teachers because we're so close to the Capital and our previous steward would sometimes travel for a meeting or to bring home books."

"What happened to him?"

"He retired when I was little, but my father still asked for his opinion for a long time."

"But not anymore?"

"He moved away a few years ago."

Adorjan leaned forward. "Tell me about Octavian."

"So you agree he's involved?"

"I never said that."

"No, but your voice changed. You do that when you shift from conversation to investigation."

He stared at her and blinked a few times. "I do?"

She nodded.

"I guess I'll never be able to fool you."

"Would you want to?"

"No."

They smiled at each other. Adorjan shifted his arm so his fingertips were touching hers. Her cheeks slowly turned red until she looked away.

"What do you think of Octavian?"

"He's very intelligent, very observant. My father lets him handle many tasks around the keep and village without direct supervision."

"Your father doesn't believe Octavian's management is in question here, from what I can tell."

"No, not at all. Of course Octavian assures my father that the blame lies elsewhere."

"I don't know about blame but I may know the cause. We found evidence that the Iron Guild underfunded a repair on the blacksmith forge in your village."

"That would explain a lot actually. I didn't know Cade Iron well. He came across as arrogant but competent. No one complained about the quality of his work. I would never have labelled him as careless. But if you know the cause why are you asking about Octavian?"

"It could be nothing more than a poorly maintained forge in which case the Iron Guild will be facing heavy fines and procedural reviews and will need overseeing for some time to ensure there is no repeat. They won't like it, of course, but safety is of paramount concern."

"To whom?"

"Pardon?"

"Safety is paramount to whom?"

"Princess Vonica."

"Right. Because she sent you here. How well do you know her?"

"Not well. I've really only known her a few weeks. But then I don't think anyone knows her well. Her stewards perhaps have known her the longest but I don't think even they know her, not truly."

Ioanna looked down at her fingernails, picking at them as she spoke. "You were one of her suitors?"

"That is how we first met, yes."

"Are you her prince?"

"No."

She looked up.

"Does that surprise you?"

"Well, she hasn't chosen a prince yet. I just thought … every suitor seems to believe …"

"She was stunned as well, but relieved. So was your brother."

"Yes, well, he cares about her, deeply. He doesn't want to see her hurt."

"It's okay, Ioanna, I guessed at the truth some days ago. I suspect without me there to muddy the water things will progress quite quickly. We may not even need the royal ball."

"Really? You think they will cancel the ball?"

"Not cancel, perhaps, but replace it with a wedding celebration. One you would be invited to and expected to attend."

She looked relieved. "That ball is my only way out of this place."

Adorjan hesitated a second. "Why do you want to leave?"

"My father will be offering me in marriage to a man I'm not interested in marrying and I will have no say in the matter at all."

"Oh, Johann said you didn't know about that yet."

"Because Johann likely found out from my father and my father hasn't told me yet."

"Then how ..?"

"I'm not allowed to visit Johann in the Capital; I'm hardly allowed to leave the estate anymore. I'm not allowed in the room when my father is handling petitions. I don't doubt they will try to separate us soon enough. The only people I'm allowed to spend any real amount of time with are my family and Octavian."

"And you think this means he has plans for you to wed you to Octavian?"

"Doesn't it?"

"Ioanna, I'm sure that your father will at least talk to you … I mean, surely even if that were true Octavian wouldn't be so bad."

"Well, I only had suspicions until now. Now I am certain." Her smile was mischievous.

"It seems you know how to get the better of me."

"Don't worry," she said, still smiling. "I won't take advantage of you too often."

"I appreciate it."

"Maybe I can make it up to you. Can I help your investigation in any way?"

"Right now there are two things you can do to help me. Can you get me into any of your father's meetings? He's proving very insistent on keeping me out."

"Go on, ask me for something difficult."

"I'm sorry, you're right. I'll figure that out on my own."

"Wait. Actually there may be something I can do. Let me talk to my father tonight."

He nodded. "Thank-you."

"What was the second thing?"

"Can you introduce me to your Hawk Master?"

13th of Thornrise 24th Year of the 11th Rebirth
Sun Temple, Sun Temple Province

Mary came in carrying a tray that smelled of honey and fresh bread to find Vonica seated on the floor with the ledger books spread around her. "You have a table," Mary said.

"It's too small."

"I can have them bring you a larger one."

"No."

Mary frowned. "Your dinner is here. And some honey cake."

"Leave it, I'll eat later."

"There's a letter here as well. Your Hawk Master says it's from Master Hearth-Glow."

"Which one?"

"The hawk came from the Sun-Song Estate."

"Adorjan then. Leave it next to my dinner."

Mary hesitated but Vonica still had not looked up. She tried one last time. "Are you making progress?"

"Yes."

Another pause. "Would you like me to summon your stewards or Master Sun-Song to assist you?"

"No."

"Then I will return later for your tray and to help you prepare for bed."

"Thank-you." Vonica still didn't look up.

Mary sighed but left. There was nothing more she could do.

Vonica stretched and sighed. A chair would be more comfortable than the stone floor but spread out like this she was able to see patterns and connections she had previously missed. The picture these numbers painted was not pleasant. She pulled herself to her feet and stretched again. Her legs were stiff and one foot tingled. At least she'd thought to grab a cushion to sit on. As she got closer to her dinner tray her stomach growled. She dropped into her comfortable chair and reached for a bun. It was so fresh it was still warm. When the bun was gone she reached for the letter.

Princess, I arrived safely at Sun-Song Estate at dinner time on the 11th of Thornrise. I was given a meal and a room for the night. Lord Sun-Song left before breakfast the next day and did not return until after midday. He locked himself in his study all afternoon and the guard would not permit me to knock on the door. As such I was not able to introduce myself to him until dinner on the 12th.

I am certain that without your letter he would have refused my offer to help and sent me on my way. Even with your letter I had to hint at your displeasure and offence if I was not permitted to stay. His reluctance vanished but Master Gold-Hearth continued to object.

Lord Sun-Song does not often join his families for meals and would not allow me to assist with anything today. I have spent most of my time with Ioanna Sun-Song learning all I can about the estate, the village, and the Sun-Song family. Ioanna is intelligent and keenly observant. She has agreed to speak with her father and hopefully gain me more access to him and the goings-on here at the estate. Her father was irate at Johann's departure and will not allow anyone to write to him. In return for her help she has asked me to include a message from her.

At this point the handwriting changed to a looping scrawl that looked more like Vonica's writing than Adorjan's.

Johann, all is well though you'd be wise not to write or visit until after the ball. When that is settled and Father accepts what we already know he will also accept that there is no need for his anger any longer. I don't know if he'll ever truly forgive your betrayal as he calls it, but it should be safe to write again after that. I miss you, brother, I hope you are well, Ioanna.

The handwriting changed back to Adorjan's neat script.

I will keep you posted on anything I discover. I hope your investigation is going well.
Adorjan Hearth-Glow

She ached to run to the library and share the news with Johann. *It hurts too much to have been so close, so sure, and have my hopes dashed.*

Instead she used the edge of the table to rip Ioanna's message from the letter and rang for Mary.

"Take this to Master Johann Sun-Song; I do not need a response."

"Yes Princess."

She finished her dinner, fetched a quill, ink, and paper from her desk, and sat down with the ledger books once more.

Something had spooked Vonica in the garden that much was obvious. Johann had felt her watching him, just as he had that first time in the library before he'd known it was the princess, and had hoped she'd come and look at what he was painting. Instead she had run from him.

He was trying to be patient but when she stopped coming to the library he went looking for her. The study where she had worked with Adorjan was empty. The guards would not let him into the private wing without a summons. He'd almost given up hope when a servant approached him with a slip of paper.

"Master Sun-Song, I have a message for you. From the princess."

His heart leapt and he thanked the girl profusely.

The princess may have sent the message but aside from one line scrawled across the bottom explaining how she had come by it there was nothing there from Vonica. It was good to hear from Ioanna and he was not at all surprised at his father's reaction, but it was not the message he'd hoped for.

That had been yesterday. Today he was convinced he could reach her, he just had to figure out the best way to approach the problem.

Maybe if I knew why she was hiding. Maybe she didn't like my painting. I didn't think she'd seen enough of it to hate it. Maybe she doesn't like artists? But she sat next to me in the library and watched me work for weeks. And even if that were the case, if she agreed with my father that artists are simply wasting their time, I'd hope she'd already like me enough not to judge me for what I do.

The word 'judge' stuck with him, nagging at him, reminding him of something.

Ah well, since I don't know what I'm supposed to remember I guess it's just reminding me that there's something more to the problem. No matter. It will come to me.

All day he pondered and schemed, but none of his ideas passed his own scrutiny. Just sneak past the guards? A good way to get thrown in a cell. An emergency message from his sister that he just had to deliver in person? It might get him in but she'd be angry when he admitted to lying. Besides, she'd read the letter from Ioanna, she would know that no one at the Sun-Song estate was permitted to write him. Write her a letter? She might not read it. She might not answer. She might not believe him. A gift? What could he give her?

His father had most likely cut him off from the Sun-Song Family accounts so there wasn't much he could afford. A painting? He had those. After her reaction to finding out he painted he didn't think reminding her of his talent was a good idea.

Maybe it's not her I need to talk to. Master Sun-Wise helped once before. Maybe he can help again.

14th of Thornrise 24th Year of the 11th Rebirth
Sun Temple, Sun Temple Province

Salazar Sun-Wise straightened his sash, brown to denote his station as steward woven with gold threads to mark his station as one of ten men honoured to serve the princesses, and gathered his records before heading for the princess's chambers. He knocked and was admitted by the princess herself. "Good-morning Princess Vonica. I was surprised that you summoned me, but glad. I've been concerned for you. Your choice to isolate yourself ..."

"Did you bring what I asked for?"

He handed over the stack of papers, quickly catching a scroll before it landed on the floor. "Yes, yes of course." He glanced around the room. There were books and papers scattered everywhere. Her breakfast tray sat on her desk, barely touched. He looked closer at Vonica and noted the dark circles beneath her eyes and the stray hair hanging down her neck. "Have you slept?"

"Some."

"You've found something?"

She nodded. "I need you to take this letter to the eyrie and send it to Rheeya in Stones Shore. It's urgent."

"Shall I send for a servant to do this so I can stay and assist you?"

"No. This is all I need. Thank-you."

"Will you be attending court tomorrow?"

"Not likely."

"Princess, I am worried about you. What happened to upset you?"

"I made an error, I misjudged myself. If you please, I have a lot of work to do."

Salazar bowed. "Of course. If you need anything else don't hesitate to call me."

"Of course."

15th of Thornrise 24th Year of the 11th Rebirth
Sun-Song Estate, Sun Temple Province

Immediately after breakfast a servant arrived and requested Adorjan's presence at a meeting. Adorjan wiped his mouth with a napkin as he stood. "Yes, of course. I'll come at once." He made eye contact with Ioanna. She smiled. He wished he could have said thank-you, or at least mouthed the words, but Lady Francesca was watching them too intently. Instead he nodded once and hoped she would understand. He could not wait for a response. "I'm coming," he said again.

Lord Yannakis, Tullius, and Octavian were already gathered when Adorjan arrived. "I'm sorry, have I kept you waiting?"

"No, not at all," Tullius said. "We were just about to begin."

"And we appreciate the princess's concerns in this matter," Yannakis added.

"We didn't realize they kept such lax hours in the Capital." Octavian kept a serious face, his posture rigid.

"I'm not sure what the princess had in mind when she sent you to us," Yannakis said.

"For this morning why don't I sit and observe your court? Over the midday meal perhaps I can offer some assistance. I would like to see more of the damage the fire caused, get out into the village with you, but of course, your duties as lord must come first."

"And when you disagree?" Octavian challenged.

"I'm not here to second guess anyone or undermine your authority. I won't say a word, I promise. You won't even know that I'm here."

He took up a seat off to the side and Octavian called for the first petitioner. Court progressed slowly. Yannakis would listen to the petition and then look to Octavian who stood next to him. Octavian would say nothing so Yannakis would ask a few questions of the petitioner and sometimes of his son and then look to Octavian again.

Octavian remained silent until Yannakis prompted him for his opinion. After the third time Yannakis said, "You're being unusually quiet today. Speak up; I rely on your aid."

"Of course, my lord."

After the petitions were heard Yannakis called for an early lunch. Adorjan touched Tullius' arm and said, "Hold a moment; I'd like to ask you a question or two, if you don't mind."

"Maybe it's best if you spoke to Master Octavian, or my father. He said …" Tullius closed his mouth, his cheeks turning red.

"What did your father say?"

Tullius shook his head. "It's not appropriate for me to repeat."

"He doesn't trust me?"

Tullius looked down.

"It's okay, I understand completely. When I was a student in the Capital I had teachers and scholars watching my every move. I thought once I became a scholar myself that would end. I was wrong. Very wrong. You can't turn a page in that library without someone checking on you. So I know, I understand. Your father is a lord and now he has a scholar younger than his heir watching his every move and checking up on him."

"Yes, that's it exactly." Tullius sounded relieved.

"You know, your father has nothing to worry about. From what I've seen your father is kind, just, and fair. I'm going to write Princess Vonica a list of compliments."

"Well, he has a way with people, but he wasn't like that with me of my siblings growing up."

"Siblings?" Adorjan said with feigned ignorance. "I've only met your sister. I didn't realize you had other siblings."

"One other, a brother, the middle child. Perhaps you've met him. He's a scholar, like you."

"I don't recall meeting another Sun-Song. What was his name? What did he study?"

"Johann, and he spends all his time drawing pictures in books."

"Ah. Illumination. No, I never studied drawing; I have no talent for it. I'm a historian myself, though I study economics and politics as well since that's more practical."

"Even that's beyond me. My teachers were always angry with me. I prefer something more physical. These meetings bore me. I'm afraid I'm going to disappoint my father no matter what happens at the ball."

They were walking now towards the dining hall. "I've heard rumours about a grand ball. I hope this assignment is over in time. I would hate to miss it."

"But you've met the princess."

"Not as a suitor."

"Is she pretty? I'd heard rumours …"

"Her scar? You can't miss it."

Tullius frowned. "I had hoped … ah well. I guess it's not important." He didn't sound convinced.

They entered the dining room together to find that Yannakis and Octavian had started without them and that Francesca and Ioanna were not in attendance.

"Shouldn't we wait for the ladies?" Adorjan said, glancing around.

"I didn't realize they allowed the female scholars to dine in the main hall. They didn't in my time," Octavian said.

"I grew up in a noble house with female relatives. My manners were instilled long before I began attending school at the temple library." He sat next to Yannakis, across from Octavian, and smiled.

"They eat later, we don't disturb them," Yannakis explained.

"Of course." He served himself. "Tullius tells me you have another son."

"For now," Yannakis said.

"Oh, is something wrong? An illness?"

"No, not unless you can cure someone of insanity."

"That sounds serious. Tullius told me he was a scholar and an artist. I'm surprised the library would admit a mad man or a fool."

"His affliction is a rather recent turn of events and caused by his association with those damned scholars. No offense. But they've addled his brain and destroyed his sense of priority and loyalty."

Adorjan spoke and moved with measured calmness. "Yes, we scholars are a single minded bunch. We dread anything getting in the way of our studies."

"And yet you are here," Octavian said. "Do you care less about your studies? Or will you be neglecting your duties in favour of your studies?"

So, Octavian is the hostile one. If I can get Lord Yannakis alone perhaps this will move quicker. He finished chewing. "Neither. I'm a student of politics. Princess Vonica does not allow viewers at court so I'm excited to have this chance to watch and learn something practical. Theory and practice are often quite different as I'm sure you're aware."

"So you're training to be a steward?" Yannakis said.

"That's certainly an option for me. I haven't decided yet. I have older cousins and brothers so I will never be the lord of our manor in the city or hold any honorary titles in other provinces but perhaps I can stand as my older cousin's steward and stay close to home." He shrugged.

"How did one so young receive so high a posting?" Octavian pressed. "That honour is usually reserved for older, more experienced scholars."

Like you? Adorjan nearly shrugged but then decided sly calculation would serve him better than nonchalance and winked instead. "It helps to have someone in your family pull some strings. My uncle is Princess Rheeya's steward so he knew right away when I would be of use to her, in a strictly business sense of course, and recommended me."

"I knew it," Yannakis said. "I should have insisted when you were a lad." He pointed at Tullius with his knife. "I should have made them take you instead of your brother. Then this whole mess could have been avoided. Now I don't know what I'll do after the ball."

"What will change after the ball?" Adorjan said. He kept his attention on his food and hoped the question sounded like idle small talk. He'd heard the just of this from Johann but he needed to hear it from Johann's father so he could judge the words and the motives for himself.

"If the priests are right Tullius will be named Prince of the Sun Temple Province. Johann is so obsessed with those books and his damned pictures that he's abandoned his family in favour of that damned library. I need an heir!"

"He's neglected his family duties and dishonoured you," Octavian said. "You are within your legal rights to disown him."

"Yes, yes, I know. I should." He sighed. "It pains me to let the estate slip away into the hands of some nephew or cousin. If I go first will they care for my widow? So many concerns."

"They may be unnecessary concerns," Octavian said. "It is rare but not unheard of for a lord to adopt a son-in-law as a legal heir so his property can be handed down to his grandchildren. Adorjan studies history and politics. I'm sure he's seen it before."

Adorjan nodded. "It is far more common among the Metalkin but it is legal and has been done here."

Now it all makes sense. Not content with his position. Well, he will be sorely disappointed when the letter arrives and Tullius keeps his position as heir. But oh, Ioanna, to be stuck with this man!

They ate dinner early and without the company of the ladies again, and then Adorjan was invited to spend the evening with Yannakis and Octavian reviewing tax records. It wasn't a glamourous job and Adorjan was more in the way than anything else but he was worried that turning the invitation down would result in no further invitations being issued. It also gave him a chance to sneak a look at some of the other records and point the conversation towards the fire at the smithy.

Lord Sun-Song seemed genuinely concerned and talked of rebuilding the village. Octavian's responses were calmly delivered but nevertheless disturbing. "I'm not sure why we need to do anything. Princess Vonica sent workers and healers; the Iron Guild will pay the expenses. What else is there for us to do?"

"It's our guards who keep the peace in the village, for our people and the workers and the healers," Yannakis said.

Adorjan got the impression it was an old argument. He cleared his throat. "Have you heard from the Iron Guild yet? I've not seen any record of payment from them?"

"No, not yet," Yannakis said. "Strange, they're usually quite prompt with tithes and taxes."

"The Metalkin hate to owe anyone money," Adorjan said.

Yannakis chuckled. "That is so very true."

"Have you ever had actual political dealings with the Metalkin?" Octavian asked.

"Yes, I have," Adorjan said. "Experience that led directly to this posting."

"What did you do?"

"I'm afraid I cannot reveal confidential information regarding a royal investigation. If you have any concerns about my conduct or qualifications you may write Princess Vonica."

"I think I will do that." Octavian stood. "Excuse me."

When he had gone Yannakis said, "Don't mind him. He's been in a foul mood all month now and I can't fathom why. Leaves early most evenings too. I don't mind. Colour me daft but I enjoy the paper work. It's steadying."

"I agree. It's a large part of why I want to be a steward."

"And for the prestige?"

"I'm sure my uncle has found prestige but most stewards go largely unnoticed. That is the nature of the job."

"You're a rare creature. Most men seek advancement and acknowledgement."

"Those aren't the same as prestige or power."

"You know, I like talking to you. Perhaps, I know you are young and without much practical experience, but the princess trusts you, so perhaps I should as well."

"You honour me sir."

"What should I do about my sons?"

"My advice is: don't disown your son. Don't do anything rash until after the ball."

"He's the rash one, leaving like a thief." The response was delivered with much heat; Johann's departure had obviously distressed Yannakis greatly.

"Would you throw away your chance at reconciliation? What does your patience cost you?"

"Perhaps a son-in-law."

"Do you want to marry your daughter to a man who only wants her so he can inherit your house?"

"I want to see her married! Octavian has served me a long time. He was a good man, if a little cold and a little strict, but a good man from a good family. Bankers, mostly, and guild leaders. A good family. He's been odd lately, colder and harder than usual, but his advice has always been sound."

"But why give him Ioanna's hand in marriage?"

"Because there is no one else. No one has offered and I have made her eligibility known. My son, he was so certain, just send her to the capital and she'd find a husband. I asked. I offered. I got no replies."

"You contacted every lord in the province?"

"Of course."

"That is unfortunate. If another, suitable options presented itself would you consider it?"

"I honestly don't know. It's getting late, friend. These papers will still be here in the morning."

"You're right. My thanks for your time today and your trust."

Yannakis nodded. "Tomorrow I will take you to the village."

"Thank-you, that would be most helpful."

"Good night."

They left the study and parted ways. Adorjan made his way back to his room where he found a letter folded neatly on his pillow.

"Adorjan, I did as you asked. You'll be spending all day with my father now. I have to apologize. My father would not have listened to me; he sees me as a foolish child, so I went to Octavian and acted all fluttery and distracted. When he questioned me I told him I could not stop thinking about you. I sighed a lot and acted like a girl in one of my mother's novels. His jealousy should keep you close to him, and my father, for the remainder of your stay. We are not likely to have any further time alone together. I hope you find what you're looking for. Ioanna."

Though it was late Adorjan sat up writing letters, one to his father, one to Vonica, and one to Johann.

16th of Thornrise 24th Year of the 11th Rebirth
Sun-Song Estate, Sun Temple Province

Adorjan took his letters down to the Eyrie. He had to get an early start as Yannakis wanted to spend most of the day down in the village talking to the builders.

"Another letter for the Princess?" Ferrand said.

"Yes and a few others."

"All right, just tell me where they go and I'll see them off."

"Have you been the hawk master here long?"

Ferrand nodded. "I apprenticed here as a lad and took over nearly fifteen years ago now. I was young then for a Hawk Master but I knew these birds."

Adorjan nodded. "So you would know about nearly every letter that's been sent out?"

"Nearly. I'm sure Master Sun-Song and Master Gold-Hearth have sent a few letters without my assistance over the years. Not to mention anything that is sent by horse and rider. Why?"

"Oh, well, I understand you have to respect the privacy of the lord you serve, but I was wondering about a rather large batch of letters Lord Sun-Song sent out."

"We've sent a lot since the fire, of course."

"No, this would have been earlier. He said he'd sent letters to every lord in the province announcing Ioanna … his daughter's eligibility. I was wondering if he sent them all at once or one at a time, waiting in between for a reply."

"Can't say I've seen anything like that at all. Most letters go to nearby estates, or are personal correspondence to the Capital. Can't remember the last time I sent a Hawk to a lord whose name I didn't recognize, and I'm not an overly learned man. I don't know all your names off by heart."

"Could Master Gold-Hearth have sent them?"

"If he did then they went out one at a time. Except for when the fire reached the eyrie, and then again after when we had so many messages to send, we haven't had an empty eyrie."

"My thanks, that puts a few pieces into place."

"No, no trouble at all. If there is anything else I can do to help, anything else you need to know, you come and ask me."

"Thank-you, I will." There was something about the intensity of Ferrand's eyes, the way he stared too hard, the way he held his hand too long when shaking it, like he wanted Adorjan to see something, to know something.

From the eyrie Adorjan went out to the stables. He could see Yannakis across the courtyard talking to two guards. He hurried to the stables where three boys were brushing and saddling the horses. Adorjan stopped one. "I need to speak to the master of the stables. Quickly."

"Of course sir, through here please."

They ducked around carpenters who were repairing the stables and stopped before a tall lanky man. His long hair was pulled back from his face. His clothes were simple but the fit and quality were better than what the boys were wearing.

"Master Clyde sir, someone to see you."

"Thank-you." He turned and shook Adorjan's outstretched hand. "What can I do for you sir?"

Adorjan noted dark circles beneath the man's eyes. "I won't keep you long. A quick question is all."

"And you are?"

"Master Adorjan, the princess sent me to look into the matter of the fire."

"And Lord Sun-Song?"

"I suppose it would be best if he thought I was here to help and not here to ask questions."

"I see. Well in that case I suppose it's best if you asked me your questions. Anything to do with the stables or the horses I can answer."

"My thanks. Repairs are moving along well?"

"Well enough. We're fortunate to be near the top of the list."

"I suppose Lord Sun-Song was relying on you after the eyrie burned down. I was wondering if he often sent out riders."

"Aside from the few we had to send while we were waiting for more hawks, no, not really."

"Anything in the last month or two? Unusually messages sent to unusual places?"

"No. Only rider out of the ordinary has been Master Gold-Hearth."

"Oh? Surely the steward of the estate is entitled to travel a little."

"Sure, sure. But he made frequent trips to the village, and the capital, for several weeks. And then at the end of Cloudrise or the beginning of Thornrise he was gone for a few days and came back right agitated. Was so bad he actually struck one of the boys."

"Did you report it?"

"No sir. Lord Sun-Song would have told me to teach the boys better manners. I deal with Master Gold-Hearth whenever possible now, but with these carpenters to oversee, well, I can only hope his mood has improved. The boy's father wasn't too happy about the bruise."

"Thank-you."

"Of course. Anything I can do to assist you, you just come and ask. Anything at all."

It sounded too much like Master Ferrand's words. He'd never questioned the servants in his own home but he was certain he'd have an easier time extracting teeth from the servants at the palace than he'd have extracting answers to any question they considered even remotely invasive.

"Master Hearth-Glow!"

"I must go. Thank-you again for your time."

Adorjan retraced his steps through the construction and joined Yannakis and Tullius at the horses. "There you are."

"Just taking a look at the repairs. Everything seems to be on track."

"I just wish they'd be quicker about it," Yannakis said. "Let's go."

"Master Gold-Hearth is not joining us?"

"No. He is dealing with some correspondence with the guilds for me this morning. Come, you wanted to see the village."

"Yes, of course." He swung into the saddle. "Lead on."

Their first stop was the site of the blacksmith's shop. The rubble here had been cleared away but no other work was being done, at least not by the builders sent by Princess Vonica. A burly man and two boys were hauling stones up to what remained of the forge.

"This is Cade Iron, our smith," Yannakis said.

"Come to show me off again?" Cade said. "I have work to do. I can't play nursemaid to every tourist from the capital."

"My son was not a tourist and they barely disturbed you. And this is Master Hearth-Glow from the Capital. Princess Vonica herself sent him here to assist us in rebuilding."

"Why bring him here? Everyone's made it clear that I'll only get help after everyone else has been seen to."

"I can't help the opinions of the other villagers, Master Iron," Yannakis said.

Cade shook his head and turned his back, going back to his work.

"I'm sorry," Yannakis said softly. "Tensions have been running high since the fire. Perhaps …"

"Father!" Tullius rode up, pulling his horse up short. "You're needed at the tents."

"Yes, I'm coming." He turned to Adorjan. "Well?"

"No, you and Tullius go on ahead. I'll catch up with you. There were some questions the princess insisted I ask."

"All right." Yannakis remounted and wheeled his horse back the way they'd come.

Tullius, still on his horse, paused. "Good luck," he said and then followed his father.

"So you're still here," Cade said. He was still working and hadn't turned.

"Yes, I'm still here."

"You're not offering to help."

"I know nothing about forges or construction; I'd only be in the way. But I may be able to offer a different sort of help if you'll gift me with a few moments of your time."

Cade stopped and looked at him. "You're not like them up at the estate. Sent by the princess?"

Adorjan nodded.

"She's not my princess."

"No, but she's working on the authority of Princess Mallory and investigating the Metalkin Guilds."

"Caden, Will, go up to the tents and help your mother with the fire wood for a bit."

"Aw Dad ..." the younger one started. The older grabbed his shirt and tugged. "Okay, we're going." They scampered off up the road.

"I don't have much hospitality to offer but I've got a low stone wall in the shade here. Tie your horse to the post and come sit a minute."

"My thanks."

"So what's this about an investigation?"

"Princess Vonica, at Princess Mallory's suggestion, is looking into the accounts of the Metalkin Guilds. We saw your request for funds, and we saw how little you were given."

"Huh. Forty gold suns is not a sum to be taken lightly."

"But it's not what you asked for."

"Been talking to other smiths in other villages. They weren't getting what they asked for either. Most though were older, already settled, or second or third generation at their forge. They had the money put away to make up the difference, or enough sway in their village to barter for what else they needed. I'm new here. Last smith left with no heirs to continue his work so the guild sent me and mine out here to take it over. I don't have that kind of gold saved up. Did the best I could with what they gave me."

"I'm betting as we go back in those records we'll find that the amount held back on each request grew because other smiths were willing to make up the difference."

"What happens now?"

"Can you write those other smiths, have them write the princess? With that information we can have the Iron Guild not only pay for your new house and forge but for the damages, supplies, and wages of the builders for the entire village."

"Would go a long way to repairing my reputation if I could get that kind of money into this village. I'll write them but I make no promises that they'll cooperate."

"That's all I can ask."

"So they're short changing everyone?"

Adorjan nodded. "I noticed the shortages in a few places, and by a few different guilds."

"Huh, and here I thought … guess it doesn't matter now."

"You had some theory as to why you were refused the money?"

"Just that I noticed something, not a shortage, the opposite I guess. I asked a few questions and was told in no uncertain terms that it was none of my business. Next thing I know my repair request comes back with little over half the gold I needed and then my forge burns down."

"Yes, very suspicious. What did you notice?"

"Metalkin trader came through with some iron, my shipment from the guild. Nothing unusual about that but he had a shipment of precious stones with him."

"From the Jeweller's Guild?"

"That's just it. Stones are transported by the Gem Guild, a Stone Clan guild. Jewellers and gem cutters tend to set up side-by-side to minimize transport costs. Mine ships 'em to the cutter, cutter has 'em run over to the jeweller to be set. That's how it's always been."

"Hmm. Very curious. And no one could answer why he had them or how he came by them?"

"Couldn't, or wouldn't. I don't know."

"I have to get this information to Princess Vonica immediately."

"So there was something to it?"

"I don't know yet, I really don't. Thank-you for your time."

"If you see my boys up there tell 'em to come on back home. They hate hauling wood."

"I will. Thank-you again."

"Master Hearth-Glow," he called after. "Anything else you need you just ask."

Adorjan stopped, one foot in the stirrup. "I will. Thank-you."

Could be nothing but then again, we weren't able to get real records from the Jeweller's Guild. So many questions, so many possibilities.

17th of Thornrise 24th Year of the 11th Rebirth
Sun Temple, Sun Temple Province

Johann waited outside Master Sun-Wise's door. The guard at the end of the hallway was watching him. He fought the urge to wave. He fought the urge to pace. He pulled at his fingers and tried to slow his heart rate back down to something normal. He'd waited five days for this meeting, he could wait a few minutes more. He took a few deep breaths and looked at the guard again. He was about to knock a second time when the door before him opened.

Master Sun-Wise and Master White-Cloud stood in the doorway. "I don't like that," Master White-Cloud was saying.

"You can't force her," Master Sun-Wise said.

Master White-Cloud hmphed and glared at Johann. "Master Scholar, don't you have business in another part of the palace?"

"Leave him be," Master Sun-Wise said. "He's my next meeting."

It amazed Johann how patient and tolerant Master Sun-Wise could keep his voice.

Master White-Cloud hmphed again. "I'm going to speak with her."

Master Sun-Wise shook his head but all he said was, "Dinner tonight?"

"A good idea."

"I'll send down for fish and you can tell me all about your discussion with the princess." Once Antony had gone Salazar turned his attention to Johann. "I expected you sooner and under different circumstances."

"I know. I need your help."

"You've said that before. Come in, please."

Johann wasn't sure if this was Master Sun-Wise's private study, which would make the door at the far end of the room the one to his personal quarters, or if it was just the one he preferred to use for business. Johann had been here before and he liked the room. It was comfortable but professional, decorated as befit a man of Master Sun-Wise's position, but not intimidating.

It's a room I can imagine myself working in, one where my wife would be comfortable sitting by the fire reading while I scrawled away on some project or other.

"So, you need my help again. What seems to be the problem?"

"She's locked herself away in her rooms."

"Ah, you noticed. I should maybe ask you about that."

"I don't know! Dammit, if I knew what was wrong maybe I could fix it."

"Maybe you were wrong," Salazar said gently.

Johann sank into a chair. "No. No, I've never been surer of anything in my entire life. I convinced you, didn't I?"

"I'm only human. Though I admit that spending time with you helped a great deal. And you never told her?"

"No."

"Not even hinted?"

"She wasn't ready to hear it. I never told her I was eligible as a suitor either."

"Why not? You were so sure and yet you didn't give her the chance to consider you?"

"You claim to know her well and yet you ask that? The whole prospect of suitors terrified her. If she thought I was trying to sneak extra time to woo her or get ahead of the other suitors she would have bolted."

"Like she has now?"

"It's not my fault! I almost told her. Before the fire. But she was running late for something; she left in a rush before I could get the words out. And then the fire and I was summoned home and she started this investigation and now I can't get near her to finish telling her."

"I'm inclined to believe that this is not your fault."

"So you'll help me then?"

"I'm not sure I can. She won't see me either. Her servant is the only person she sees now."

"Then disguise me as a servant."

"Only females are allowed to wait directly on the princess. It has been that way for nine rebirths."

"Let me guess, a suitor trying to get more time with the princess?"

"Most likely."

"Can I wash the floor in the hallway so I can catch her when she leaves her room?"

"She hasn't left her room in days. There's no need."

"None at all?"

"She has her own privy chamber. A servant brings her meals and runs her letters. She has enough room to work and a bed. She has access to both a private garden and a private chapel without ... now hold on, there's an idea."

"What? What is it?"

"The chapel. Vonica's private chapel. Technically I or Antony can use it as well. It's cleaned by an acolyte not by Vonica's private servants."

"But how do we know when she'll be there?"

"We don't, and I make no promises, but maybe with a little prompting I can arrange things, but on one condition."

"Yes, anything."

"When you speak with her you must tell her the truth."

**18th of Thornrise 24th Year of the 11th Rebirth
Sun-Song Estate, Sun Temple Province**

"Are you certain of this?" Ioanna asked.

"No, not certain at all. There may be nothing there. Princess Vonica may not be able to defend us if you are caught."

"That's not very reassuring Adorjan."

"I'm sorry. I don't lie very well."

"You'd better lie well or we'll be caught for sure!"

"Oh, well, that's different. I cannot lie to you. Are you ready?"

She held up her mother's keys. "As ready as I'll ever be. Now you'd best go before father gets suspicious."

Adorjan nodded. He gripped the scroll a little tighter and marched down to the dining room. At the door he paused, took a deep breath, and smiled wide. He flung the door open startling the men already at the table.

"Adorjan, what is it?" Yannakis asked.

"A letter, my lord, from the Princess. I simply must share with you some of the contents."

"Surely such communication is private," Octavian said.

"You'll understand when you hear it." He took his place between Yannakis and Tullius, unrolled the scroll, and began to read words that were not there.

"Your letters have filled me with great hope for the well-being of my people. Lord Sun-Song sounds like a capable and just ruler. Over the course of my investigation I have encountered so few men like him. I sincerely hope that one day I will have the chance to meet him in person and thank him for his care and dedication."

"She really said that?" Yannakis said.

"Oh yes," Adorjan said, lying through his teeth.

"Hold a moment." Yannakis waved a servant over. "Fetch my wife at once. I want her to hear this." He turned to Adorjan. "You don't mind, do you?"

"Of course not," Adorjan said. *Just don't call for your daughter or all this will be for naught.*

Ioanna crept through the hallways, listening carefully for servants, or worse, Master Octavian. The steward's quarters weren't far from her own room and she knew the way well. As a child she'd spent time there, learning to read at the table in the small study. But the steward who had advised her father when she was young was long gone. She hadn't been back in these rooms since Octavian had taken the position.

She looked over both shoulders then stuck the key in the door. She disappeared inside the room and closed the door softly behind her. When she turned around she gasped. The room was almost bare.

The book shelves had been stripped of books and ornaments. The tapestry was missing from the wall. The carpet in front of the hearth was missing. The furniture was there but the vase was gone from the table. Ioanna frowned.

Footsteps in the hallway spurred her on. She glanced back at the door then hurried through to Octavian's bed chamber. This was also bare of everything but the necessities. It struck her as odd but at the same time made searching his belongings that much easier.

She started in the desk and almost gave up when she came across a locked drawer. None of her mother's keys opened it. She searched through his dressing table and found no key. What she found instead was a small glass vial with a cork in the top. The cork had once been sealed with black wax but the wax was broken and the vial empty. She rolled it between her fingers, studying it.

The door opened.

She shoved the vial in her pocket and ducked down behind the bed. She listened to the footsteps out in the study and the rattle of dishes. Then the steps came closer. She could see the servant picking up clothes. If he turned around she was caught.

He didn't turn. Instead he fussed with one of the robes and set something hard on the desk before going out with the laundry.

Her heart was pounding like a jack rabbit with a fox on its tail. She was ready to flee, to apologize that she couldn't find the papers, but the item on the desk caught her eye.

It was the key.

She snatched it up and fumbled the desk drawer open, looking over her shoulder the entire time. She rifled through the papers until a Metalkin seal caught her eye. She glanced at the papers as she pulled them out, taking only the ones that might be useful.

She stuffed everything in the pocket of her dressing gown and headed for the door. She had her hand on the handle when it opened.

Octavian stopped in the doorway, staring at her. "Miss Ioanna, this is a surprise. Just what are you doing in my rooms?"

"I was concerned that your evening tea was not made properly. I was ensuring that everything had been done right. And I thought I would leave you an extra biscuit." She smiled sweetly.

"Thank-you for your concern. Would you care to stay and have tea with me?"

"That would be lovely but mother is expecting me for dinner shortly. And it wouldn't be proper. Another time, perhaps."

"Another time then."

She slipped passed him into the hallway. She glanced back. He was standing in the doorway watching her. She smiled and waved before continuing on her way, forcing herself to walk normally. Only when she heard the door close behind her did she allow herself to run.

They met in the library that evening after Yannakis and Francesca turned in for the night. Ioanna watched Adorjan flip through the papers she'd found, her eyes still bright from the excitement. "So? Are they important? Will they help?"

Adorjan nodded. "It's something at least. Depending on what Vonica and Johann have found this could help a little or a lot. I will send it to the Capital in the morning."

"You'll need to send a rider," Ioanna said. "I also found this." She handed him the vial.

"What was in it?"

"I don't know. Maybe it has nothing to do with the investigation. It's not very big. I don't think it could contain something that would start a fire, not one big enough to burn down a forge."

"No, you're probably right about that. Still, I'll send it along. Should your father ask after me in the morning tell him I've gone to speak with the Hawk and Stable Masters."

"Will I be lying?"

"No. They both sounded eager to help. These papers have left me with a few questions about Octavian's messages and travel habits that they may be able to answer."

20th of Thornrise 24th Year of the 11th Rebirth
Sun-Song Estate, Sun Temple Province

Vonica looked over the contents of the package from Adorjan again. The messenger had arrived late the night before claiming it was urgent and Vonica was glad she'd insisted the man be admitted. Aside from the letter of explanation the package contained a stack of papers and a small vial.

The letters had contained an accounting of Octavian's debts along with some vague communications between him and someone at the Jeweler's Guild. Vonica would compare the letters to the information she'd been gathering later, right now it was the vial that had her attention now. She rolled it between her fingers, much the same way Ioanna had done a day and a half prior. "What was in it?" she mused. It was so small, too small to hold a drink or tonic. "A powder or medicine to be mixed with something perhaps?" Vonica knew nothing about medicines but she knew exactly who to ask.

Rebecca Vines-Grace was the palace hearler and perhaps the oldest person Vonica knew, except maybe Master Royal-Gold at the Jeweller's Guild. When she knocked on the door to the healer's suite a young girl opened it and then curtsied.

"Princess Vonica, it is an honour to welcome you. Please, come in."

"Thank-you. Is Madam Vines-Grace available?"

"Soon. She is just in the healing room. A minor issue, she will be out soon. Please, sit. May I fetch you tea?"

"No rush, but I'm sure Madam Vines-Grace and I will want some while we talk."

"Of course."

After a few minutes Vonica was admitted into a cluttered sitting room. The girl was setting out tea while Rebecca dried her hands.

"Princess Vonica, what brings you to my end of the palace? Not an illness I hope?"

"No, I am here for advice."

"Of course. I will provide you with whatever knowledge or wisdom I can."

"When you trained to be a healer you learned all about what plants and such could heal a person, and which could harm them, correct?"

"Yes. And you would be surprised how many can do both."

"You keep a lot of medicines on hand, correct?"

"Yes."

"How do you store them?"

"I have jars, shelves and drawers of them. Is there one in particular you have questions about?"

"Yes. Which one would you store in a vial with a black wax seal?"

"Black wax you say?"

"Yes."

"Hmm. Undyed wax is used for most things. We use a red wax for things that must be handled with care. Black is only used for things best left alone. Wherever did you come across a vial with a black wax seal?"

"One was discovered in the course of our investigation into the bank and guilds." She produced the vial and handed it over to Rebecca who accepted it gingerly.

"I can see no trace of what was in there, but I can tell you it was dangerous."

"What can you tell me about Master Maceo Heart-Flame, the archivist at the Merchant's Bank?"

"Only that he is dead and that it was very sudden." She handed the vial back.

"So you did not assist him?"

"No. One of the senior healers in the Capital saw to him. I received a letter, asking for my opinion. The healer thought the death was too sudden, or not sudden enough. You see, when a death is natural, it is instant or it lingers a predictable amount of time. This came on too quick and lasted too long. I'm not sure that makes sense to someone who has not studied these things. Unfortunately Master Heart-Flame was old, nearly as old as I am, and his family simply wanted to mourn his passing."

"So there is nothing else you can tell me?"

"What I can tell you is that you should ask Master Green-Rivers in the city for his opinion. And you should show him that vial."

Master Green-Rivers arrived after the midday meal and bowed deeply when Mary showed him in. "Princess Vonica, I never dreamed I would receive a royal summons. How can I be of assistance to you?"

"Thank-you for coming so promptly. I have some questions for you."

"Of course. Ask away." He dropped into the offered chair with a flourish of his hands.

"What can you tell me about Master Heart-Flame?"

"He should not have died. His fever came on so suddenly, too suddenly, and then he lingered in pain for days. If I had known the cause in time, something he ate perhaps, I could have saved him.

There was time. But there were too many things it could have been and not enough time to test for them all."

"Something he ate? Or something he was fed?" Vonica handed over the vial.

Madam Vines-Grace had handled the vial as if she were afraid some trace of whatever it held might harm her. Master Green-Rivers snatched the vial from her hand and held it up to the light, twisting it this way and that, almost eagerly.

"Yes, this must have contained something not intended for human ingestion. You think this vial is somehow connected to Master Heart-Flame?"

"I don't know. It was found in the possession of a man with steep debts who made a trip to the Capital around the time Master Heart-Flame died. This man is now close to clearing his debts and stands to marry well. But I have no proof that one thing is connected to another."

"Proof I cannot give you, I'm afraid. The Heart-Flame family insisted on taking the body away for cremation. There is nothing more I can tell you, and nothing more we can hope to learn from him. May I take the vial with me?"

"I would hate to lose it."

"I shan't lose it, or damage it. I think that if I were to dip it in a tea made from … no, the concoction's recipe would mean nothing to you. Suffice to say there is a discolouration to the glass here and if it reacts the way I think it will react then we will have some idea of what this vial contained."

"Then I will await your findings. Thank-you."

The letter and vial arrived that evening. Vonica set her fork aside with a shake of her head. "Why am I surprised by this? He didn't seem like a man to rest when there was something interesting to pursue."

"Is there anything else you need, Princess?"

Mary had left early that afternoon and Vonica found she wasn't nearly as found of this girl. She shook her head. "No. That's everything for now."

She opened the letter. It was short and messily scrawled but direct. The vial had contained poison. He could narrow it down to the family of plants but could not name the plant specifically nor could he tell if it was a powder or liquid they were searching for. What he did know for certain was that if he was correct in his identification this plant produced symptoms identical to those Master Heart-Flame had suffered.

Is this proof enough? How can we possibly find more?

**21st of Thornrise 24th Year of the 11th Rebirth
Sun Temple, Sun Temple Province**

Vonica opened the reply from Rheeya with trembling hands and was surprised at the bold handwriting. Once she got past the list of titles she discovered why the writing looked odd.

I, Evan Fire-Stone, steward to Rheeya Stone-Rose, am honoured to address your questions. There has been no official investigation into the Iron Guild in our province. I am certain, given the contents of your letter, that you have heard stories or rumours regarding certain events at an iron mine in our province. I can assure you that the matter is well in hand and does not threaten the balance the princesses are sworn to uphold. We are confident this issue will turn out to be a misunderstanding between the Iron Guild representative and the uneducated, low-born, overseer at the mine. He will be removed from his position for causing this trouble. Such is only fitting.

As for your concerns over the actions of the Merchant Bank, there have been no complaints. The bank is not at all involved in the current altercation at the iron mine. Is there a problem we should be made aware of? Accusations against the bank are a serious business and I hope you have spoken to your stewards about the political implication of such accusations.

If you have any further questions do not hesitate to contact me, Master Hearth-Glow, or Princess Rheeya. We will answer you with utmost haste.

I hope your quest for a prince is going well. Many of these disruptions could be solved if you and your fellow princesses completed your soul bonds. It is not my place to admonish you but your neglect of duty will harm the entire island.

Vonica clenched the paper in her fist. She wanted to burn the damn thin but a small voice of reason told her she might need it.

Deep breath, think. If you'll get no help from the Stone Clan you'll have to do this yourself. Just set everything in order and send a copy to Mallory first. This would be easier with Johann's help. No. You can't ask him for help. You're on your own and you have to work fast, before Evan Fire-Stone writes a letter to Antony. I'd best send for Adorjan.

22nd of Thornrise 24th Year of the 11th Rebirth
Sun-Song Estate, Sun Temple Province

Adorjan had escaped his duties these last few days simply by telling Lord Sun-Song the truth. He'd found something important and sent it to Vonica and until he heard back from her there was nothing he could do but wait. Of course he'd expected her reply much sooner. Not that he minded. He was spending his time in the library with Ioanna again.

She had been reading him passages from her favourite books and asking all the questions that had burned inside her, some he answered, some he had to admit he didn't know the answer to. Either way each question sparked a marvelous conversation between them, the type of conversation that meanders from topic to topic until he sometimes wasn't sure he'd answered the original question.

This morning her questions were less academic. "Tell me about the Capital, about the library."

"Do you really want me to tell you? Wouldn't you rather see it for yourself?"

"More than anything, but …"

A knock at the door interrupted her. "Master Adorjan? A letter."

"Come in," he said.

The servant entered, handed the letter over with a bow, and backed out.

"What is it? Bad news?"

He showed her the seal, a rose in full bloom surrounded by sun rays. "I doubt it. Probably my new instructions. What were you saying about the library?"

"We've talked about this. I'll never see it."

"It's so close, Ioanna. You'll get there. I promise."

"How can you possibly promise that?"

"I'll take you there myself," he insisted.

Now she laughed.

"Why is that funny?"

"And how will you manage that when my father forbids it?"

He blushed and broke the seal on Vonica's letter. He glanced down at the words and nearly dropped the page.

"What? What is it?"

"Since I am done my investigation I'm to return to the Capital. It's early enough that if I leave now I can be back before dark."

"Now?"

He nodded. "She's quite clear in her letter here. Unless I've discovered something new in these past days I'm to return. She needs my help putting all the information we've gathered together. Apparently what you found was important."

"What about ..?" her cheeks turned a bright and rather charming shade of pink.

He reached out impulsively and took her hand. "Ioanna, I know why your father forbade you from leaving here, and I know who is behind it. I will not let this happen to you."

She turned away. "You got what you came for and now you're leaving and I'll likely never see you again."

"My duty calls me away but my heart longs to stay here with you."

She turned and grabbed his hands. "Take me with you to the Capital. Now. Please."

"It's midmorning. How would I sneak you out? Besides, your father would accuse me of abducting you and his letter would beat us to the Capital by hours. The guards would be waiting."

"Lie like you did before. Tell them the princess summoned me."

"And if your father asks to see the letter?"

"Please, if you care for me as you are implying don't leave me here."

"I don't want to but she is the princess and he is your father. We both have orders to obey. Expect a letter, or two, in the next few days, that will fix everything. I promise."

"Letters? From whom? How can you be sure?"

"One will be from my father, it is late. One will be from Vonica." He did not mention that, in his opinion, that letter was late as well.

"Adorjan, do you love me?"

"With all my heart, I swear it."

"Then I must trust you. Please, don't make me wait too long or my father will order me to marry Octavian." She stood, kissed his cheek, and hurried away.

22ⁿᵈ of Thornrise 24ᵗʰ Year of the 11th Rebirth
Sun Temple, Sun Temple Province

The note was tucked between the teapot and her favourite cup. "What's this?" she said to Mary.

"It's from Master Sun-Wise, M'Lady. He requested I deliver it to you this morning."

"When did he give it to you?"

"Last night, but it was late, I had only just returned. He said it was important but not urgent enough to wake you. I swear, I didn't read it."

"It's all right. Thank-you."

"Is there anything else I can get you?"

"No, that will be all."

The note was short and not at all what Vonica expected.

Princess, I know this investigation is putting a lot of stress and pressure on you. Remember, even when the answer is not clear to you it is clear to Airon. Perhaps it is not my guidance you need now, but his. Master Salazar

Had he been watching the chapel? Did he know she hadn't been to pray in over a week? No, not likely, not by the sound of this letter. The tone was gentle, not chiding.

As she sipped her tea she thought, *Adorjan said something similar. Perhaps he's right. Perhaps I just need to clear my mind.*

She finished breakfast and sat staring at the pile of books and papers, the letter from Master Green-Rivers near the top. She felt sluggish, heavy. She looked out at the garden and the chapel beyond. *Yes, I definitely need a break.*

Johann felt ridiculous. He had traded in his fine robes and scholar's sash for a plain hooded robe in heavy, undyed cloth.

"You'll be posing as an acolyte sent to clean the chapel," Salazar explained in the wee hours of the morning. "You'll sweep up the ash from the incense, clean dried wax off the floors, remove candle stubs and place fresh candles …"

"This is servant's work."

"A servant is anyone who serves, Master Johann, and that's what priests do, they serve Airon. Acolytes come from all walks of life. Some have never made a fire or fixed a meal. These jobs teach humility and service."

"I understand. I'm sorry."

"Very good. You'll want to do each task slowly. I can nudge Vonica but I can't command her. Master White-Cloud has been trying that for months and it has finally blown up in his face. I don't know when she'll go to pray so be patient."

"I've waited this long for the chance. I guess I'll have lots of time to pray as well."

Johann was surprised when the door to Vonica's private suite opened so early and Vonica stepped into the chapel. He stepped back into the shadow behind the Stone Spirit altar but he needn't have bothered. Vonica's gaze stayed glued to Airon's shrine. There was a low bench in the middle of the chapel but Vonica remained standing, her weight shifting from foot-to-foot in a slow, nervous fashion.

He took a deep breath. *Okay, don't startle her. Just let her know you're here and …*

She took a deep, shuddering breath and began to speak. "I don't know what to do; I don't even know why I'm here. This whole thing with the guilds is a mess. I'm finding so many errors, both in records and in judgement. Are they errors? Or are they a sign of something more? Something darker? Princess Mallory urged me to look into this because of what happened at the iron mine but then Princess Rheeya had her steward reply to me to tell me nothing was wrong. She didn't even write to me herself. Why did she do that? Why didn't she write back to me? She always has."

She paused and took a few breaths. When she began again her voice was calmer, softer. "I thought I loved him. Oh, Airon, how could I have been so stupid. Only an illuminator? Ha. Even if I didn't guess at the beginning I should have known when I found out he was noble born. An artist? A painter? Is that some sort of cruel jest? Why would you do that to me?" Her voice broke and she turned and fled back to her room leaving Johann alone again.

He stared after her. *Did I hear her correctly? She's in love with me? I have to see her, have to tell her.*

He had his hand on the door when the one behind him opened and a voice said, "What are you doing? That part of the palace is off limits."

Johann turned, careful to keep his face down. "I'm sorry. I'm new. I got turned around. It won't happen again."

"No, it won't. Report back to your superior immediately."

"Yes sir." On his way out he glanced back. He'd seen this man before, a few days earlier. He'd met with Master Sun-Wise. Master Sun-Wise had called him Master White-Cloud, Vonica's other steward.

No wonder Vonica complained about him so often. Still, damn his timing. I suppose I'd better inform Salazar Sun-Wise of our failure. At least now I know what is bothering her.

Adorjan handed the reins of his horse over to the stable boy. It was late, the sun, which had spent most of the day behind thick grey clouds, was already setting, and he was worn out from a hard day on the road.

"Master Scholar, allow me to help you with your bag."

Adorjan looked up, blinking owlishly, expecting a servant. "Johann?"

"Adorjan. I heard rumours you were returning today." The grey sky began spitting rain drops on the courtyard. Johann grabbed the travel bag. "And just in time. Come on, before the rain really starts."

Though his legs were tired Adorjan was glad of Johann's urgings and they made it inside just before the droplets turned to a steady downpour.

"Have you eaten?"

"Barely a thing since breakfast."

"Did my mother serve sweet rolls while you were there?"

"Yes, on more than one occasion."

Johann sighed. "Of all the things I'll miss about not seeing home again, those sweet rolls are high on the list. Did you learn anything useful?"

"Your father hasn't disowned you yet, and I don't think he will."

Johann nodded. "Sounds like we have much to discuss. Is my sister well?"

"As well as can be expected. She'll be better soon."

"Oh?"

"I plan to marry her."

Johann's whole body drooped, his expression becoming one of anguish.

"I'm sorry. Have I offended you?"

"No. I am happy for you, truly. I'm afraid I will never be as lucky as you."

"I was curious about that. I had expected good news sooner rather than later."

"Seems it will be never rather than sooner. I had a meal brought to my room, if you don't mind the cozy quarters."

"It's fine, my own is no bigger."

When they had settled at the table, their knees practically touching, Adorjan said, "Do you love her?"

"Yes, and today I discovered that she loves me as well, or so she confessed to Airon. But she doesn't believe anyone could love her because of that damn scar. How do I make her see past that hateful thing?"

"I don't know."

"I'd take it if I could," he said, his voice softening. "I'd wear that brand the rest of my days so she could be free of it."

"If only it were possible. Though you could pray for it."

"I have. Many times." He sighed. "That's why I was waiting for you. I had to tell you, warn you."

"What?"

"She's locked herself away. She's not herself. She's giving up. I can't even get in to see her."

"She called me back. If she sends for me I'll bring you with me."

"I don't know."

"We have to try. She has to see you again."

23rd of Thornrise 24th Year of the 11th Rebirth
Sun Temple, Sun Temple Province

Adorjan and Johann made their way together only to be stopped down the hall from Princess Vonica's door. The guard held out an arm to stop them.

"I'm Master Adorjan, the princess requested my assistance."

The guard nodded. "Of course sir, she is expecting you." He held out an arm, halting Johann. "Just you."

"He's with me."

"I'm sorry, the princess was very specific."

"It's okay," Johann said. "Go on. I have other things I need to do."

Adorjan nodded. He found Vonica in the study sorting papers. "Princess Vonica, I see you've been busy while I've been away."

"Adorjan!" She looked up and smiled at him. "You're back. Good. The news is not good I'm afraid."

"No, it's not. But what have you discovered?"

"The vial you found contained a harmful plant extract. It can be used to treat fevers if mixed correctly. I doubt Master Gold-Hearth has the knowledge to do so."

"No one at the Sun-Song estate mentioned a fever going around. So if Octavian was not sick and was not educated in the proper use of the contents of the vial, why did he have it?"

"To poison Master Heart-Flame."

"Now that is an accusation you must not speak aloud to any but me."

"I know."

"The healers?" Adorjan pressed.

"They don't know where I got the vial from."

He nodded. "Do you have any proof, aside from the vial?"

"Not enough. Why would a steward employed at an estate a day's ride east of the Capital want to kill the archivist of the Merchant Bank?"

Adorjan shrugged. "I don't know. Why? Weren't there any answers in the papers I sent you."

"Take a look. This is what I've pieced together." She handed him a stack of papers, notes she had taken while working.

He sat down and started reading. At page three he stopped. "Wait, here, this part about the Jeweller's Guild. Cade Iron mentioned seeing a Metalkin merchant transporting gems and noting that it was odd."

"Hmm. That explains the gap here." She grabbed a ledger from the bank. "There is no record of payment from the Jeweller's Guild to the Stone Cutter's Guild in over four months. I thought perhaps the money was changing hands in other provinces. So they are buying the gems in other provinces and moving them on their own."

"And the records from the Jeweller's Guild? What do they show?"

"They are still missing."

"And still no word from Master Royal-Gold?"

"None."

"Have you written the Stone Cutter's Guild?"

"I dare not. Master Fire-Stone wrote on Rheeya's behalf. Apparently I do not have her support in this."

"Damn. Let's see what else we have. With enough proof we could force her cooperation. What about the Iron Guild? The repair shortages?"

"There's no way to prove the other shortages caused any problems."

"The other smiths didn't write you?"

"I received nothing from them. Unless …" She called for a serving girl. "Fetch me Master White-Cloud, and tell him to bring all the letters that arrived in the last nine days."

"Yes Princess."

"What are you thinking?" Adorjan said.

"Just that the letters may have gone to my steward's desk along with all the other complaints."

"I meant about all of this. What happened? Where did this start?"

"Start? I don't know. But we know it ended in a fire." There was a knock at the door. "Come in."

Antony came in and bowed without dropping a single paper, miraculous considering how many he was carrying. When he straightened Vonica could see he was out of breath. "Here is everything you asked for, My Lady. What are you looking for?"

"Reports or complaints from any black smith in the province."

"Yes. There were a few in the last few days and I found it odd. Generally the guilds handle these things internally. We only deal with issues involving people of different provinces."

"I know. I asked for these men to send me their reports."

"For your investigation?" Antony said. He seemed to take a step back from her without moving.

"Yes. This may be exactly what we need."

"I see," Antony said coolly. "Is there anything else you need from me?"

"No, just leave us the letters, all of them, and we'll sort them out."

"Of course. My lady, Master Hearth-Glow." He bowed and left empty handed.

"He still doesn't approve?" Adorjan said as the door closed.

"No. And I don't think he'll like what we've discovered. But even he could not expect us to keep this quiet, if we find the proof we need."

"Talk out what you know, maybe we'll catch something we missed."

"Cade Iron saw a suspicious shipment of gems and probably questioned it. Later he is short-changed on repair funds and then his forge and home burn down, damaging his village and ruining his reputation."

"Yes, but we have no proof of any connection between those events."

"Then we have Octavian. He's acting oddly and made a trip to the Capital around the time Master Heart-Flame fell ill."

"To be fair Ioanna mentioned their previous steward made frequent trips to the Capital. And I spoke to the Stable Master at the Sun-Song Estate; he confirmed that Octavian made frequent trips to different estates and to the capital as well."

"Then the timing could be coincidence. From the papers you and Ioanna found we know he has debts and that he made a substantial payment towards them after Master Heart-Flame died."

"Again, there's nothing linking those two except coincidental timing." Adorjan didn't like making excuses for Octavian but he had to be fair.

"He was in possession of the vial."

"Which we cannot definitively link to Master Heart-Flame's death."

"And we suspect he failed to send multiple messages his sworn lord ordered him to send."

"And we know Lord Sun-Song trusted Octavian alone with the house accounts."

"Do we know why didn't he send those letters?"

"He wants to marry Ioanna. Perhaps he thought the only way he could win her hand was by eliminating all competitors."

"You want to wed her too; I'm not sure desiring a woman as your wife is a crime."

Adorjan's eyes went wide. "And he counselled Lord Sun-Song to disown Johann."

"But why?"

"He's putting himself in line to inherit Sun-Song estate. I realized that early in my stay but I didn't know about the debts at the time."

"There's no crime in wanting to improve your station," Vonica said.

"Not unless he does something illegal to achieve it. The letters. My father can confirm that he never received on. Ferrand Hound can confirm he never sent them. Is that enough to have him dismissed?"

"Not by me. Only Lord Sun-Song could dismiss him for that."

Adorjan turned for the door. "I'll write him tonight."

"No."

"What?"

"No. Not until we know what's going on, what's really going on. If he suspects we're investigating him we may lose our chance."

Adorjan sighed. "You're right, of course." *I'm sorry Ioanna. I am trying.*

After a long day of sorting papers and making lists they had traced out a web of errors that were too neatly aligned to be just clerical mistakes. The threads tied the Iron Guild, the Jeweller's Guild, and the Merchant's Bank together over and over again. Adorjan added another account to the list at hand and stretched.

"Vonica, we need a rest, some food. We'll miss something if we keep going at this pace."

"All right. I'll send down for some dinner. Chicken tonight?"

"Vonica, let's eat in a dining room. Maybe Johann could join us. I'd like his opinion on a few things we discussed."

"I don't want to waste time with a long meal. I'll eat here."

"Then I'll eat with you. How goes the planning for the royal ball?"

She pushed the ledger back. "I've put it off this long. I don't think I want chicken. A roast?"

"Yes, that sounds lovely." He waited while she addressed the servant. "You really don't want this ball, do you?"

"Of course not."

"Can I offer you some advice?"

"I think I'd rather your advice than my steward's."

"I don't know what happened while I was away but we need Johann's help. This concerns his family. He's intelligent and loyal to you and eager to help. Please, stop shutting him out."

"He has his own job. I've wasted enough of his time."

"He doesn't see it that way."

"We've got this in hand. And I don't see how completing this investigation faster will put an end to the royal ball."

Adorjan sighed. "Of course. Forgive me." *It seems I'm not doing a good job of helping any of my friends today.*

31st of Thornrise 24th Year of the 11th Rebirth
Sun Temple, Sun Temple Province

My Dearest Vonica,

My deepest apologies for not writing sooner. I have been away from Stones Shore and have only just received your letter. Evan assures me he responded promptly but given all that has transpired here I worry that he may have misled you.

Yes, I am investigating the Iron Guild. Jared Iron-Smith, a representative of the Iron Guild, has been arrested for treason among other charges. It's quite the story. I've included some account information I think you will find useful. You also have my permission to question any of the Stone Clan guilds if you think it will aide you. I have no reason to believe they are involved in any way, but I'm sure Mallory thought the same thing about the Iron Guild.

The rest of the long letter chronicled Rheeya's adventures at the Black-Mountain estate and in South Bay in her familiar, casual tone. Assassination attempts, cave-ins, two misunderstandings about the identity of her prince, one harmless and humorous, the other very nearly disastrous, Dark Spirits; Vonica sighed wistfully, it all sounded like a story in a book.

"And I am stuck staring at ledger books all day. At least I'll be leaving for Shores Stone soon." She set the letter aside and finished her dinner. Adorjan had left early to speak with Johann. She felt a twinge of guilt whenever she thought of him but she pushed it aside. "Tomorrow we get some answers."

32nd of Thornrise 24th Year of the 11th Rebirth
Sun Temple, Sun Temple Province

The list of invitations went out as soon as Vonica finished eating. She'd requested over three dozen officials, clerks, and archivists from the bank and three guilds present themselves at midday. It was short notice but then she hoped she'd stirred up the nobles enough that they wouldn't dare refuse such a prestigious and rare invitation.

One by one the men were to be called before Vonica and Adorjan while Antony hurried about offering reassurances to the ones still waiting and trying to hide the fact that he knew nothing about this.

The first interview was perhaps the most emotional for Vonica and she watched the stately gentleman approach the throne, waiting until he was at the foot of the stairs to address him.

"Lord Heart-Flame, thank-you for seeing me on such short notice."

"An honour Princess."

"May I offer my condolences on the passing of your uncle?"

"My thanks, My Lady."

"Did you bring the documents I requested?"

"I did."

Vonica nodded to Adorjan who went down and collected the papers.

"I'll just review these quickly so you may take them with you again when you go," he said.

"Certainly. Ah, may I ask why you were interested in my late uncle's personal papers? You don't think he was ... That is to say I've heard rumours of your investigation."

"Your uncle is not suspect in our investigation, but I believe that, had I been able to speak with him on this matter, the investigation would already be over."

"I see." He looked relieved.

"Tell me, do you know a Master Octavian Gold-Hearth?"

Lord Heart-Flame frowned. "My uncle worked with several Gold-Hearths but I was not familiar with them. Lord Gold-Hearth runs an estate south of the Capital if I'm not mistaken."

"Did your uncle talk about work at all?"

"Only in generalities, and usually to complain. Too many stairs, slow clerks, that sort of thing."

"Did he meet with anyone in the weeks before his passing?"

"His work was solitary. His wife died in childbirth a great many years ago. My cousins are grown, most working in other provinces. He kept a room at the family estate and we were honoured to assist him but I think he preferred to be alone. It had been a great many years since he accepted any form of social invitation."

"What about the thirty-fifth of Cloudrise?" Adorjan said.

"I'm not sure. That was two months ago. No wait, I don't know if it was that day or not, but he was late for dinner one day, said an unusual request had kept him late at the bank. It could have been the thirty-fifth. Did you find something?"

"Perhaps. How soon after that odd request did your uncle fall ill?"

"Within days. How did you know? What did you find?"

"What we were looking for," Adorjan said. "I'll need to leave tomorrow." He brought the papers over to Lord Heart-Flame. "Thank-you for these."

"Of course. But I'm afraid I don't understand."

"Explanations will have to wait until the investigation is complete. Thank-you again for coming."

Lord Heart-Flame bowed. "Of course. I am always honoured to serve."

When he was gone Vonica said, "So you have proof?"

"I have proof they met just days before Master Heart-Flame fell ill and there were some notes there regarding the nature of the meeting."

"I'll review it tonight. We have other questions to ask yet today. Tomorrow I will send Sir Cyril and a proper escort with you to the Sun-Song estate."

"Good."

"Tell them to send in the next man. Start with the Stone Cutter."

The guard brought in a small, stocky man with grey hair. His features were prominent on his round face and he appeared almost trollish. He bowed, a simple gesture, and said, "Master Hearth-Stone, representative of the Stone Cutter's Guild, at your service, Princess Vonica. And it is an honour to meet you."

"Thank-you for coming. How is business these days?"

"To be honest, Princess, business is non-existent, or so it feels most days. There are rumours from home that Princess Rheeya has found her prince and the guild masters here are hopeful that will bring an end to this slow season."

"And in the other provinces?"

"Slow as well, though not as bad as here."

"So you've had no recent dealings with the Jeweller's Guild?"

"No, Princess. And not only that but fewer gems are being found. There was always a fear, you see, eventually we would find every precious stone on the island. They do not grow back like trees or wheat or goats."

"Of course. I hope that is not the case. I have always wondered: how closely do you work with the Jeweller's Guild?"

"Intimately. Perhaps more closely than any other guilds work together."

"What's the procedure then if I wanted say a brooch made?"

"For any piece there are two ways it can be created. Sometimes the jewellers request a stone cut to a specific shape and size to fit a setting he is working on. Other times he will craft the piece around a pre-cut stone."

"Does he make adjustments to the stone?"

"No. The setting is more flexible and easier to adjust to minute differences."

"Could they though?"

"Princess, there is very little stopping any of us from exploring jobs outside the realm of our specific spirit guides. Perhaps a Stone Clan smith or a Metalkin potter would not be as naturally gifted, perhaps their craftsmanship would never reach master statues, but it could be done. Only tradition really prevents us from trying."

"That is certainly food for thought."

"Was there anything else?"

"Yes. Do you know of any guild shipments being carried by Metalkin merchants?"

"No, Princess. I suppose a jeweller somewhere else could purchase the stones and hire whomever they please to transport the shipment for them."

"Yes, of course. Thank-you. If I think of anything else I shall write you."

"I hope I helped."

"You did indeed."

Vonica took a few deep breaths as he made his way out. "Well, Adorjan, are you ready for the real work to begin?"

"I think so."

She nodded. "Send in Master Quinton Golden-Heart."

Quinton entered with his son in tow. He bowed grandly. "I am honoured by your invitation, Princess. May I introduce my son ..?"

"No, you may not."

Quinton's smile faltered. "My Lady? I thought ..."

"I'm sorry; I have many important interviews to complete today. Master Hearth-Glow, would you show Master Golden-Heart the list of errors you discovered?"

"Errors?" Quinton took the paper. "What is this?"

"Errors we found in your ledgers. It looks like money is being lost. I wonder where that money is going."

Quinton frowned. "I don't like what you are implying."

"I'm implying nothing. I am asking you to explain these errors. I'm assuming there is an explanation for them."

"Of course there is. They are simple clerical errors."

"Clerical errors. I hope you will fire those clerks. Large sums of money are simply missing from these accounts. How will the people get their money back? And how did these errors slip past notice?"

"Perhaps it was past time for Master Maceo Heart-Flame to retire from his position of archivist."

"Blame a deceased man," Vonica murmured. "You claim to know nothing of these errors?"

"It is not a claim. I know nothing. I had no part in it and I guarantee that no member of my family had any part in whatever you're implying."

"Then I charge you with the full review and correction of all the records. You personally, not a clerk under your supervision will ensure that all the accounts held here are balanced. I'll not have it said that we are not upholding our part of the pact."

Quinton bowed deeply. "Of course, Princess. Whatever you command, I shall see done."

"And you will report to me every fourteen days until the task is completed to my satisfaction."

"Yes Princess." He bowed again. "Yes Princess, of course."

"You are dismissed for now but do not go far. After the testimony of the others I may have more questions for you."

Another bow. "Yes, yes of course. Come Barron." Father and son left quickly.

"Shall I call the next master banker?" Adorjan said.

"No. Call in the clerks first. A few subtle threats should suffice to make them reveal who was ordering the accounts tampered with. We'll get further with them than we will with the masters."

Though most of the clerks they spoke with were twice named it was evident from the quality of their clothes and the nervous way they held themselves that they were the younger sons of younger sons with no hope of a title or large inheritance. Aside from being able to trace their bloodline back to some lord or other they were really no different from the common born merchants and bankers they worked with.

They bowed low, too low, and had to be prompted to speak up. Interviewing Master Golden-Heart first turned out to be less of a mistake than Vonica first thought. The threat of losing their jobs seemed to be familiar to them and they readily believed that their superiors had placed all the blame on them. Once they got over their initial shyness their testimonies simply poured out.

"We are watched constantly," one said. "Our mistakes are caught even as we're putting pen to paper."

Another explained, "Those accounts are for the guilds, or the guild masters' personal accounts. We don't work on those accounts; they claim we are not careful enough. And if we do work on one of those accounts we are not permitted to enter anything into the ledger. We do the accounting separately and present it to the masters."

"They tell us what to write. If we question or protest they threaten our jobs. If we tell anyone they will certainly put us on the streets and our fathers will disown us," said a third. He was cringing as he spoke.

Vonica showed them the books, asked for names, promised them safety and security, and they talked. So did the clerks from the guilds, all with similar stories.

"That's the last of the clerks," Adorjan said. "Shall we start calling in the guild masters?"

"Do you think we need to?"

"It will look odd if we dismiss them without speaking to them first."

"I wasn't planning on dismissing them. Call them all in, and Master White-Cloud as well."

"And Master Golden-Heart?"

"Yes, him as well. I have another task for him."

It was odd to see so many people in the hall at one time and for once Vonica was not nervous. They weren't all staring at her. Mostly they were glancing at each other.

"My good sirs, thank-you for coming on such short notice. It seems I have gotten all the information I need from your clerks."

"So we're free to leave?" someone said. "We have work to do."

"Actually, I would like you to remain here a little longer," she said with a smile.

"How much longer?"

"Five days."

"Princess," Antony said, running forward. "Is that really necessary? These are important and busy men."

"It is necessary I'm afraid. There is one other I wish to speak with and my assistant here must go and fetch him."

"But surely they can wait at home," Antony said.

Vonica ignored him. "Master Golden-Heart, it seems I have one more task for you to do for me, one that must be done before the end of the day."

Quinton stepped to the front of the group. "Of course, Princess. Anything."

"I need you to freeze the accounts of every man in this room, and all the Metalkin guilds."

The noise level jumped from nothing to overwhelming instantly. Vonica waited calmly until their protests died down.

"Princess Vonica," Antony said. "Are you arresting these men?"

"No, of course not. I am detaining them until I can conduct the trials. They will be given a room in the guest wing of the palace."

"You don't mean to throw us in the dungeon?" someone near the back of the group said.

"Of course not. None of you have been charged with a crime. You are critical to this investigation and I would hate for any of you to be called away on other business suddenly. No, it's best you stay here as my guests until the trial can be completed. Master Golden-Heart, you are free to leave as you have work to do. Master White-Cloud please see that each of our guests is settled. That will be all for today." She stood. The men scrambled to bow as she walked out with Adorjan at her heels.

"That was artfully handled," he said.

"Can you imagine the uproar if I had called for the guards?"

He chuckled. "Yes, that would have been amusing. Still, you were wise in your decision. Now, I must pack, and I must speak to Johann and my father before I leave tomorrow."

"Will you be joining me for dinner tonight?"

"No. I'll likely be eating with my parents. I'll see you in the morning."

"All right. I'll speak with Sir Cyril and write your letters for you."

"Until tomorrow then." Adorjan gave a little bow and went on his way. He went to Johann's room and knocked twice.

"How did it go?" Johann asked as he opened the door.

"You should have seen her. It was amazing. I leave tomorrow."

"You're returning to the estate?"

"Yes. And if all goes well I will not be returning for the trial. She will not be able to hold this trial without allowing an audience so you'll be able to watch."

"Thank Airon for small blessings then," Johann said. "I have a letter for my sister; will you take it with you?"

"Of course I will. Have you eaten?"

"No, it's not quite dinner yet."

"We had our midday meal early. No matter, I'll wait and eat with you. I could use your opinion on a few things."

"If you're going back there does that mean you found evidence against Octavian?"

"Enough to force his confession, I think, if I play it right. That's why I want to talk to you."

"You may know more about him than I do. He didn't start working for my father until after I was living here."

"Then we'll brainstorm together."

34th of Thornrise 24th Year of the 11th Rebirth
Sun-Sung Estate, Sun Temple Province

Adorjan approached the dining room with what felt like stones churning in his stomach. He'd arrived after dinner the day before and had been greeted by Yannakis in the courtyard.

"When you asked if I'd consider another offer for my daughter's hand you failed to mention it was you who was interested," Yannakis had said, clapping the younger man on the shoulder.

"Then my father's letter arrived?" Adorjan said.

"Yes, only a day after you left. I was wondering when you'd arrive. Everyone else has eaten already but I waited on you."

Adorjan had wanted to tell Yannakis everything right then but most of it had to wait until the interrogation was complete. He declined Yannakis' offer to a drink and turned in early.

Everyone was seated at the table and the servants were just setting out the food. He couldn't have timed it any better. Yannakis rose. "There you are. I thought I'd have to send someone to fetch you."

"You surely don't mean to make the announcement now," Adorjan said.

"Why wait any longer?"

"Because, my lord, I have serious business to discuss with you."

"Later Adorjan, your business will have to wait until we deal with this."

Adorjan bowed his head. "As you say my lord."

When everyone was seated again and the servants had gone Yannakis said, "My darling Ioanna, you are grown now and it is one of my duties as your father to find you a suitable husband."

"Yes Father."

"I have had a proposal for your hand and have accepted it."

"You've always been a kind parent, and fair, I'm sure whomever you've chosen will be suitable."

"So deferential! I'm sure I'll be facing that strong will of yours again soon. Well, at least now there is another to share the burden of your opinions. And in my opinion, he deserves it. And he deserves you. He has served our family well. Ioanna, I'd like to introduce you to your soon-to-be husband."

"My lord," Octavian said, getting to his feet. "You do me a great honour."

"Oh sit down, Octavian," Yannakis said.

"What?" Octavian stammered. "But I thought …"

"Ioanna my dear, it seems you have stolen Master Adorjan's heart. He's asked for your hand and I've given my approval."

"Thank-you Father," Ioanna said, keeping her face lowered. She glanced over at Adorjan and smiled. He smiled back.

"Well, this is very good news indeed," Francesca said. "Adorjan, you must take some time and familiarize me with your family before the wedding."

"Of course. But first there is some pressing business …"

"Tomorrow," Yannakis said. "I'll be keeping you busy today; you can return the favour tomorrow."

Adorjan suppressed a sigh. "Yes sir."

Adorjan was on his way back to his rooms to wash up for the midday meal when Octavian cornered him in a corridor. "Master Hearth-Glow, a moment of your time."

"A short moment. Lord Sun-Song has me running today."

"You've quite the entourage with you this visit. Any special reason?"

"My father was not happy I chose to travel alone last time and sent me with a guard this time. He is concerned about Dark Spirits I suppose."

"There has been no report of Dark Spirits in our province and in the other provinces they are in the wilder regions, not within a day's ride of the capital cities."

"You know that, and I know that, but we both know that fathers can be overbearing sometimes and the best thing to do is agree with them."

"I don't know what you're up to …"

"I met a young woman who stole my heart. I discovered her father was looking for a husband for her so I had my father write regarding my interest, and then I left it in Airon's hands. I haven't done anything wrong."

"I'm watching you."

"Good. Don't look away. I wouldn't want you to miss anything. Excuse me; I'll be late for the meal."

True to his word Yannakis kept Adorjan busy with introductions and paperwork and a hundred other things all day. It wasn't until after dinner that Adorjan was able to slip away to speak with Ioanna in private.

He opened the door to the library to find her reading. He knocked lightly to announce his presence.

She looked up and smiled. "Adorjan." They met halfway and he wrapped his arms around her.

"Didn't I promise?"

"My father is not a patient man. What if your father's letter had come days later?"

"It didn't. You're going to be Madam Hearth-Glow just as soon as we can get this wedding planned."

"That could take months."

"It could, especially with this investigation."

"You have to leave again?"

"No. I shouldn't have to leave now for a few weeks. My part in all this is nearly done."

"Oh, thank Airon. Will we live here, afterwards? Or will we live in the Capital?"

"Either way I will take you to the Capital to see the library, and to meet the princess. I promise."

She tucked her head under his chin and leaned against him and sighed. All the worry, all the stress, melted away. Her father had made a decision and she knew from experience that it would take a lot to change his mind.

35th of Thornrise 24th Year of the 11th Rebirth
Sun-Song Temple, Sun Temple Province

Octavian arrived for breakfast at the usual time to find Francesca and Ioanna seated at the table. "Good morning Lady Sun-Song, Lady Ioanna, you're eating early this morning."

"Yes, we have a busy day ahead of us," Francesca said.

"Is your husband joining you this morning?"

"He had pressing business this morning and said he wasn't hungry. Will you be joining us?"

"I think perhaps I should

"I'm sorry Sir but you can't go in right now."

Octavian glared at the guard. "I'm the steward of this estate."

"Yes sir," the guard replied. He wore the Sun-Song crest but Octavian didn't recognize him. "But I still cannot let you in. Lord Sun-Song is hearing a special petition."

"And it's my job to advise him."

The door opened and a second guard stuck his head out. "Lord Sun-Song wants you to fetch – Master Gold-Heart, how fortunate. I was about to send for you. Lord Sun-Song wishes to see you."

Octavian gave the guard at the door a smug smile and marched into the hall. "I'm sorry my lord, I didn't realize we were beginning so early." He paused to take in the scene before him. Two more of the estate guards stood at the door just behind him. Yannakis sat in his usual seat with Tullius at his side. Adorjan stood before Yannakis and just off to one side with a tall, fair-haired man in light armor. There were four additional guards in the room wearing the same light armor marked with the royal crest. "I've missed something important it seems."

"No, it is I who has missed what is important. And to think I once counted you a friend," Yannakis said.

"My lord, I don't know what you're talking about."

"Go ahead Adorjan."

Adorjan nodded. "Octavian Gold-Hearth, when you met with Master Heart-Flame what did the two of you discuss?"

"We discussed some personal financial matters. Why?"

"You discussed your personal finances with the bank's archivist?"

"Yes."

"So you did not discuss the shipment of precious gems through this territory?"

"We have no mines here, nor a jeweller. Why would we receive shipments of precious stones?"

"I didn't say they were being shipped here, I said they were being shipped through here and you didn't answer my question."

"No, we did not."

"That's not what his notes on the matter state."

"Master Heart-Flame was old and apparently ill, though he hid it well. I'm not sure that his notes are entirely trustworthy."

"Yes, it seems to be common right now to blame the dead man." Adorjan reached into his pocket and pulled out the vial. "Perhaps you would rather explain how you came into the possession of a vial of poison, or what you used it for?"

"That did not contain poison. It was medicine. I was not well while I was in the capital and saw a healer."

"It's been examined by a healer." Adorjan pulled out a second vial still sealed in black wax; a gift from Master Green-Rivers. "The healer was able to identify the contents and provided me with a second sample. Since it is just medicine I'll have Tullius fetch you some water and we can mix this up for you. I'm sure you won't mind proving ..."

"No!" Octavian fell to his knees. "My lord, do not make me drink. I swear, I will tell you everything."

"I don't want to hear everything," Yannakis said. "Are you confessing to putting the contents of the vial in Master Heart-Flame's drink?"

"Yes." He buried his face in his hands.

"Then you can save your story for Princess Vonica. It is she, not I, who will oversee your trial."

Adorjan waved to the guards. "Sir Cyril, you may take him away now. The princess will want to speak with him as soon as possible."

Cyril nodded and two guards grabbed Octavian, hauling him to his feet. "We'll take our leave then, my lord."

"Yes, yes. Just get him out of my sight," Yannakis said with a wave of his hand. When the room had cleared of guards he said, "I suppose I will need to review the house accounts. Airon only knows how much he stole from us. And to think I was about to let him marry my daughter. I owe you a great debt, Adorjan. I'm not sure Ioanna's hand quite covers it."

"Sir, I was doing my duty, nothing more."

"Still, I have need of a new steward, unless you are bound in service to the princess?"

"No sir. I had planned to stay a while to spend time with Ioanna. I'm sure both she and the princess would approve of my staying here. That is, if you are offering me the position."

"I am. I'll need someone to assist with the mountain of paperwork this mess has created."

"Then I would gladly work for you, sir, and for your son in the future if he is pleased with my work."

Tullius crossed the room and clapped Adorjan on the shoulder. "We're to be brothers, you can drop the formalities. I'd be glad to work with you."

"First thing's first," Adorjan said. "I will need to write the princess and fill her in."

"Make it quick. We'll be busy for days."

1st of Daggerrise 24th Year of the 11th Rebirth
Sun Temple, Sun Temple Province

Adorjan's prediction had been accurate. For the first time in ten years the hall was full. Extra benches had been brought in and still people were standing. Johann found himself a corner where he could just see the front of the room and hoped he wouldn't be too noticeable.

Vonica came out with her stewards and took her place at the top of the stairs. "Bring in Octavian Gold-Hearth."

Johann hardly recognized his father's steward. Since he no longer held the office of steward he was no longer permitted his green sash. His hair was dishevelled and there were dark circles beneath his eyes. When the guards released him he dropped to his knees.

"Princess Vonica, I wish to confess to you everything I know and I throw myself at your mercy."

"Stand and speak," Vonica said. "Tell me what you know."

"I am ashamed to say that I made some poor choices as a younger man, choices which resulted in my being cut off from the family accounts after which I fell into debt. I begged my family for assistance and they helped me secure the position at the Sun-Song estate. Still, I had my debts to deal with and my wages were hardly making a dent in them. Because of this I was desperate and leapt at the chance to make some extra coin."

"Who gave you this chance?"

"A Metalkin trader whom I met on the road between the Capital and the Sun-Song estate. He told me he was looking for someone who could help him move precious stones through the estate's village without being noticed. He needed to sell them to someone so the next trader could come and purchase them. I agreed to act as the middle man and they promised me a percentage of the price. This helped for a time but still my debt shrank too slowly for my liking.

"I received a letter asking me to assist with a problem they were having. Someone at the bank was asking questions about the accounts and the movement of these stones. I was given the vial with the next shipment of stones and was told to present myself at the bank on a certain date. When I arrived I was to act like I too was suspicious. In this way I was to confirm if this person was truly a threat and if he was I was to pour the vial in his water."

"Did you go through with this plan?"

"I did. It wasn't until I reached the bank that I discovered the identity of the man I'd been sent to speak with. Master Maceo Heart-Flame."

"Did you use the vial?"

"Yes."

There was a roar from the gathered nobles and Vonica had to wait for her stewards and guards to return order before continuing.

"And after that?"

"I was paid, a lot. It paid off a substantial part of my debt. I was not involved in the fire at all, I swear it, but after the fact I made sure that the blame fell squarely on Cade Iron's shoulders. With his reputation in shambles no one would believe him if he started talking about the gems he saw."

"Do you know where the gems came from?"

"No Princess."

"Do you know who else was involved?"

"There were two men at the bank who helped with the arrangements. A third was in charge of the accounts. I will give you their names. I swear, this is all I know."

Vonica turned to her stewards. "This man has confessed to murder, among other charges. What is your advice? What should I do with him?"

"He is in debt, Princess," Salazar said. "There is no money to seize, no way for him to make reparations. His family has already cut him free. They are not involved in this at all and cannot be made to bear the weight of this new debt."

"He must pay," Antony said. "He confessed to taking a life, and to corrupt business dealings. If it was just the gems I would say a hefty prison sentence would be enough, but to kill a man to hide your crimes? And to do it for money? This is severe."

"How long a prison sentence?" Vonica mused.

"Several years at least," Salazar said.

"His entire life, possibly," Antony added.

Octavian trembled and buried his face in his hands.

"Lock him up for now," Vonica said. "When the trials are over we shall decide how long his sentence shall last, or if something more severe than prison is required. Master White-Cloud you will go with him and collect the names of his accomplices and then have the guards escort them here. I will deal with them next."

9th of Daggerrise 24th Year of the 11th Rebirth
Sun Temple, Sun Temple Province

The trials lasted seven days. On the eighth Vonica stayed locked in her room at turns buried in her bed sobbing and sitting at her desk writing letters. This morning she felt calmer, but only as long as she didn't think about what lay ahead.

She was dressed and waiting when Antony knocked on her door. "I see you're ready," he said. "Let's get this over with."

"Antony, this had to be done."

"Then finish it."

She bowed her head. Even with the inescapable evidence he was still disappointed in her.

The hall was already full. Vonica took her seat and waited for silence to descend. "Thank-you for coming today. Many of you were witness to the proceedings of this court. Reports have already been sent to the other princesses. The five Metalkin who were found guilty of crimes in our province have been fined and are being sent to their own province under guard. Princess Mallory Jewel-Rose will sentence them further if she sees fit.

"More concerning are the seven officials at the Merchant's Bank who have been found guilty of accepting bribes, altering accounts, and other fraudulent practices. When Airon set our island free of the invaders from across the sea he commanded his princesses to keep the balance, to keep the peace. At that time certain boundaries and duties were set. We are responsible for the histories of this island and we are responsible for the economic stability of this island. That is our role in the pact.

"The corruption that was discovered in the Merchant's Bank threatens the balance and anything that threatens the balance threatens the pact. This makes something as simple as changing a number in a ledger book a serious crime. All seven officials have been stripped of their position within the bank and their titles. They no longer hold the honour of being twice-named, nor do their wives or their children.

"They have been fined and punished. They have lost their jobs, their families, and their prestige. This is deemed to be suitable punishment for their crimes. As such I am freeing them as soon as all of their fines have been paid in full."

Vonica took a deep breath and glanced around the room. There was tension among the nobles but also a sense of relief. "There is of course the matter of Octavian Gold-Hearth. Murder is a serious crime. This is not a case of a brigand on the road. This was premeditated. Master Heart-Flame was targeted because he had become suspicious of this corruption. I know Master Heart-Flame's family is demanding justice and vengeance.

"Octavian has lost his position as steward of the Sun-Song estate and has been stripped of his second name. His possessions have been sold to repay his debts and even that was not enough. He is to be imprisoned in the palace dungeons in a solitary cell and put on the most basic of rations for the remainder of his days. He will be allowed no visitors and no favours. When he dies he will be cremated as is our custom and his ashes buried among the commoners' graves, no place for him will be saved in the Gold-Hearth crypts. This is my ruling on this matter."

As was expected there was some muttering and murmuring from the crowd. She had debated this sentence for hours. No matter what she did there would be some who cried it was too harsh while others demanded a harsher payment. In the end she simply could not bring herself to order Octavian's death.

"There is the matter of my prince," Vonica said. "There have been rumours and I wish to put them to rest. Master Adorjan Hearth-Glow was extremely helpful in the course of this investigation but he is engaged to another. I will be leaving in three days' time for Shores Stone to celebrate Princess Rheeya's wedding and upon my return I will decide how to proceed with my duties of finding my prince. There will be court tomorrow but I will not allow an audience. There will be no court on the eleventh. That is all."

She'd been in court less than an hour but she felt ready to return to bed for the rest of the day. Instead she went to the study and boxed all the ledgers, sorting them by guild. She had servants collect them so the guards could return them to the guilds. To each box she added a letter of thanks for their cooperation.

With that taken care of she returned to her room to find a letter waiting for her from Adorjan. She had Mary bring her tea and settled in to read.

11th of Daggerrise 24th Year of the 11th Rebirth
Sun Temple, Sun Temple Province

Quinlan Golden-Heart had a son, two nephews, and a second-cousin on the suitor list. His wife, sister, sister-in-law, and father's cousin were all nagging him to get their sons in to see the princess, as if he had any control over it. He was lucky the princess's investigations had only landed him a mountain of paper work and not a place in jail as it had seven other low-level officials. Today he had finally been granted an audience with Master Antony White-Cloud.

He'd dressed for the occasion, hoping his fine clothes would encourage Master White-Cloud to take his concerns seriously. Still, he felt nervous as the servant, a girl of about fourteen, led him to the study. She was common born, about the same age as his youngest daughter, probably the daughter of palace servants. At best her father was a guard. But she carried herself with dignity. She didn't meet his eyes for more than a moment, to do so would have been rude, but she didn't cower either. *Even the young servants are as comfortable around lords and bankers as my own daughter. Of course they are. They deal with the royal stewards all the time.*

He was surprised to find the study no fancier than his own back home. The carpets were nicer and the upholstery on the chairs a better quality but otherwise it truly looked and felt like home. He took a deep breath and tried to relax.

Antony White-Cloud came in only a minute behind him. "Forgive me, I didn't mean to keep you waiting."

"Not at all, I only just arrived myself. Thank-you for seeing me."

"Of course, Lord Golden-Heart."

"My father is still Lord Golden-Heart. Master Quinton is formal enough for me."

"All right, Master Quinton then. What can I do for you today?"

"I'm deeply concerned. The meetings with the princess were cancelled more than a month ago and we've still received no word on when the meetings will resume, or when this royal ball we've all heard rumours about will be held. And now this news from Stone's Shore. Princess Rheeya is getting married this month."

Antony replied with practiced calm. "You're not alone in your concerns friend. Every noble family with eligible sons has asked the same. I'm sure you know better than most how much time this ordeal with the Merchant's Bank and the Metalkin Guilds took up."

"Yes, quite distressing to discover the corruption hiding right under our noses. We will remain diligent going forward."

"Of course."

Quinton squirmed slightly in his chair.

"Of course it is my firm belief that the lack of a prince in our province played a large part in allowing the corruption to sink as deep as it did. The soul bond maintains balance, as you know. I'm surprised we are not plagued with more complaints of Dark Spirit attacks in our province. It must be the devote practice of our priests that keeps us safe." As he talked Quinton nodded along. "You are right, however, that something needs to be done, now that the investigation is out of the way." He sighed. "Princess Vonica is leaving for the wedding tomorrow and doesn't return until the twenty-fourth."

"Surely that's enough time to plan a royal ball. You already have the guest list."

"You would think so but it is a royal ball and therefore everything requires royal approval. Without that, I can do nothing."

"I was hoping for better news, a concrete date."

"Yes, I understand that. I will notify all the families as soon as I know something, I promise."

"Yes, of course. Very good."

"Was there anything else?"

"No, and I don't want to waste your valuable time." Quinton stood. "My thanks again."

Antony stood and shook Quinton's hand. "I'll walk with you a ways. My next appointment is with a priest across the courtyard. My job requires a lot of walking."

Quinton put both hands on his stomach. "This is the cost of a relaxing desk job, this and tired eyes."

Antony laughed. "Then I will be grateful."

They parted ways at the main door under the watchful eye of a stony-faced guard. Antony smiled as he walked across the courtyard. He'd had a dozen such meetings these past few days, all with the same results, and he was feeling justified in the decision he had to make.

The priest, a weasel-faced man with a rich, kind voice that didn't suit him at all, was waiting just inside the entry of the priests' dorm He smiled but it was strained. "Master White-Cloud, you made it."

"You said you had news for me?"

"Yes. When Chief Priest Gold-Spark was preparing to leave for Stone's Shore he mentioned something about the new prince that I thought you would find interesting."

"Yes, yes, go on."

"Did you see the invitation?"

"Of course."

"And you didn't notice?"

Antony let out an exasperated huff. "Notice what?"

"Thomas Mason. The prince has only one last name."

"I thought it was an error. So, a merchant's son perhaps?"

"No. Miner. Thought I heard he managed an iron mine."

"Commoner? Low born commoner? Are you certain?"

The priest nodded. "And High Priest Gold-Spark didn't seem concerned at all, as if it didn't bother him that one of the five most important titles in on the Isle of Light hadn't just been handed to a miner."

"That settles it. We must host this ball as soon as Vonica returns. I can have everything planned and ready for approval by the time she returns from Stone's Shore."

12th of Daggerrise 24th Year of the 11th Rebirth
Sun Temple, Sun Temple Province

She left the letter on her breakfast tray, grabbed her cape, and went out without looking back. Her wheel-house was in the courtyard harnessed to four white horses. There were guards and servants milling about. Salazar appeared at her elbow. "Master Antony and I will take care of things here for you. I think this trip will be good for you. To see Rheeya again, you need that. You two were always close."

"Yes, I do miss her."

"It will be a longer journey, going through the mountains. From here to Golden Hall is so much closer. I envy you this excursion. It's been twenty-five years since I last left the Capital."

"I didn't realize. Is there somewhere you wish to go?"

"My place is here and I'm content. Travel is for younger men. I don't much relish the idea of sleeping on the ground or spending eight hours in a saddle. No, I will stay here, thank-you."

"Princess, we are ready for you," said Sir Cyril.

"Yes, I'm coming."

Vonica and Mary had been gone two hours before a servant got around to cleaning her rooms and found the note and another hour before the note made its way to Johann.

Johann, I hope you will forgive me for running away from you in the garden. My apology is a long time coming, and I can no longer hide behind the investigation or the trials. I should have said something sooner. I know you offered to help, and I know you tried to talk to me about it, but I needed space. I needed time to accept some things and try to forget others. I am leaving for a few days for Rheeya's wedding. When I return I hope we can resume our meetings in the library when my schedule allows. I have missed the books and our conversations. Vonica

After reading it he tucked it away in a safe place. *Ha. She offers me friendship. Well, I'll take what is offered gladly. I will have to show her that my friendship and my love are not so different and hope she can accept it.*

17th of Daggerrise 24th Year of the 11th Rebirth
Stone's Shore, Stone Clan Province

Vonica stretched as she exited the wheelhouse. She expected the flurry of guards and servants around her but she hadn't expected the young, red-headed woman who rushed out the main doors to greet her so promptly.

"Vonica!" Rheeya embraced her friend. "I've missed you. Letters are not enough."

"No, they are not. Congratulations."

"Thank-you. It was quite the adventure."

"So I surmised from your letter. Are the other girls here?"

"Betha and Taeya are. They're in the solar visiting. They've been inseparable. Mallory is due to arrive later this evening so we shall have tea and catch up." She linked arms with Vonica. "You have to tell me more about this investigation and the two young men who were helping you."

"Oh, it's nothing like that," Vonica said as Rheeya led her towards the castle.

They had a late dinner that evening: Rheeya and Tomas, Mallory and Kaelen, her prince, Vonica, Taeya, and Betha. The girls talked and laughed; even Mallory, who had not grown up with them, and Tomas, were easily drawn into the fun, adding tales of their childhoods.

Just after the soup course Rheeya said, "I know you're hovering just outside the door. You're just getting under foot. You might as well come in here."

A boy of eight appeared in the doorway. "I was trying to stay out of the way." His voice was innocent, almost pleading, but his eyes darted everywhere with obvious excitement.

"I could hear them scolding you. Never mind, you're here now. Fetch the stool from against the wall and set it next to Tomas."

He went quickly before she could change his mind.

"Who's this now?" Kaelen huffed.

"This young man is James Quarry. He is a distant relation of Tomas' and he lives with us here. After the festivities he'll begin his schooling," Rheeya said.

"Why here?" Kaelen pressed. "Why isn't he with his parents?"

Mallory was staring down at her lap. Rheeya's face had gone hard. The boy, James, just smiled. "Oh, I don't have parents anymore." He glanced at Tomas then added, "Sir." He looked around the table. "They don't look anything like you, do they?"

Taeya and Vonica blushed. Mallory looked up again, suddenly curious. Betha grinned.

"We're not twins," Rheeya said.

"Common rabble," Kaelen muttered.

Vonica, who was on the other side of Kaelen, glanced his way, shocked. Luckily no one else seemed to hear. In fact Mallory was smiling.

"Tell me James," Mallory said. "What will you be studying?"

"Dunno yet. To read I guess. Rheeya thinks I could be a steward, or the Captain of the Palace Guard. I hope they teach me to swing a sword."

"Excuse me," Kaelen said. He pushed away from the table.

"Where are you going?" Mallory said.

"To our quarters." He flashed a quick, forced smile in Rheeya's direction and left.

Betha put a hand over Mallory's and glared at Kaelen's back.

"Can I have something to eat?" James said.

"I thought the cook was feeding you in the kitchen," Tomas said.

"She did. I was too excited to eat much."

Rheeya and Tomas smiled over his head at each other. "All right. Help yourself."

"Is there going to be dessert?"

"Later." Rheeya couldn't keep the laughter from her voice.

The servants brought out the main course and a quick word to one of them had an extra plate on the table for James.

"Who helped you with the frogs?" James said, peering intently from one face to the next.

"You told him about the frogs?" Betha said, her eyes going wide.

Taeya was blushing.

"What frogs?" Mallory asked.

"Oh, when they were all girls …"

"James, I'm not sure we need to discuss that now," Tomas said.

"Aw, but she asked. And she's a princess."

"Later. You can tell her later."

"Really? So I'll get to talk to her again?"

Vonica thought Tomas looked tired.

"Rheeya, were our provinces the only ones affected by this recent upheaval?" Vonica said.

"I'm still investigating," Mallory said. "Unfortunately no one is willing to work with me. The guild masters keep telling me I'm going about things wrong. 'That's not how it's done'. I swear, that's all I hear. My steward, Conrad Old-Silver, he tells me to be patient.

He insists I study more and meddle less. I have an entire education that no one here has but because I don't know your history and traditions they all consider me a fool. It's beyond frustrating." She stopped talking suddenly and blushed. "I'm sorry."

"It's okay," Betha said, "We over share all the time."

"At least you found your prince," Taeya said with a dreamy sigh. "He can help you settle in."

Mallory shifted in her seat. "Yes. I guess he's supposed to."

"It's natural to miss your home," Tomas said. "And to feel a bit like a fish out of water. Believe me, even though I grew up on the island, in this province, all the ceremony and tradition is foreign to me. In time, we'll find our way."

"Thank-you, Tomas."

"Rheeya," James said. "Is it time for dessert yet?"

Rheeya sighed with gusto. "Later."

18th of Daggerrise 24th Year of the 11th Rebirth
Shores Stone, Stone Clan Province

The wedding was being held at midday while the sun was highest in the sky. Vonica had an early breakfast alone in her quarters and Mary assured her the other girls were doing the same. "Everyone knows it will be a whole day of visiting," Mary said. "Nothing wrong with wanting some time to yourself first."

Vonica ate and washed and then sat on the low bench in front of a dressing table that was not her own while Mary fussed with her hair.

"You're going to put it up, aren't you?"

"We had this argument at Princess Mallory's wedding. You must wear it up, it's tradition."

Vonica sighed and turned her gaze away from the mirror.

"I've been thinking, ever since you were sobbing into your pillow," Mary said.

"Thinking about what, exactly?"

"Your scar. You hate it."

"Of course I hate it, it makes me ugly."

"Perhaps it does, perhaps it doesn't. I don't think that's important really."

"Oh?"

"We used to talk about you back home in my village. I bet you didn't know I wasn't from the Capital. I've lived there a long time, been honoured to serve, but I still go home when I can. I was young when it happened, young and not yet working at the palace. One of the others came home and it's all anyone could talk about. We all asked so many questions."

"It's all everyone talks about, or stares at. Why didn't they just tell everyone what happened? Then people wouldn't ask."

"Know what they say about you?"

"Ugly, scarred, a disappointment."

"Blessed."

Vonica scoffed. "Me? Blessed? By a scar?"

"We are all blessed by your scar. We have the strongest princess in the history of the pact. Touched by Airon's divine fire, chosen by Airon himself. The child who survived, who witnessed firsthand the fullness of Airon's power and lived. No other princess could boast such a feat. All the villagers agree. We are all blessed because you are strong."

"I don't feel strong."

"None of us do, not all the time. But you can be strong. You've shown your strength when you stood up to the guilds, to the bank."

"I can't, not this time."

"Why not?"

"I allowed myself to hope that finding my prince would not be impossible after all but I was wrong."

"How can you be sure?"

"Artists love beauty and perfection and no matter how strong this scar makes me I am neither of those things."

"Some will see you exactly as you say, Princess, that can't be helped. I pray Airon will give you the strength to see yourself differently. Now, up with you, I need to get you dressed."

It was difficult to pay attention. High Priest Gold-Spark could be an interesting man, it wasn't his fault the prayers were so tedious, nor was it his fault that Vonica's thoughts were wandering.

They're happy. Anyone could see that. Rheeya hasn't stopped smiling. I want that. Airon, I want that happiness so much.

After the service they had dinner. Vonica was expecting a party but the list of dinner guests fit in the same dining room as the evening before. All the princesses, and Prince Kaelen were there, along with James and a middle aged man with a minor limp who was introduced as Tyson Mason and could only be Tomas's father. Two other couples were seated at the table and were introduced as Lord and Lady Black-Mountain, their son Dwayne, and his new wife.

The atmosphere at dinner was light-hearted and casual. The laughter was loud and frequent. Betha, whom many people found blunt and even rude, was making Lord Black-Mountain roar and slap the table.

James had managed a seat next to Mallory, to Kaelen's obvious disgust, and from her sudden squeals of delight he'd managed to tell her the entirety of the frog story without Tomas or Rheeya catching on.

Vonica smiled. *I must remember to tell Johann about James.* Thinking of Johann made it even more difficult to enjoy herself. And thoughts of him came often. A book recommendation from Taeya she thought he would also enjoy. A childhood story Rheeya shared that she told herself she must share with him when she returned home. Halfway through dinner she was feeling homesick.

As servants were clearing away the second course Lord Black-Mountain stood. "Not long ago we were blessed to have Princess Rheeya present for the engagement and wedding of our son and she did us the honour of saying a few words. Now it is my honour to return the favour. I've known Tomas since he was a boy and he's always been a good lad. Had I known he was going to grow up to be my prince I may have let him off lighter for that incident with the stolen cart."

Tomas went red right to the tips of his ears.

"I can say that I have never seen a better match in all my years. Peace and prosperity will return to our province, now that the two of you have found each other. But more importantly, the two of you have found happiness, and you deserve it."

"Here here!" Dwayne shouted, raising his glass.

"To Princess Rheeya and Prince Tomas!"

Everyone cheered and drank and refilled their glasses as the next course was served.

Vonica turned in right after dessert. Mary helped her take all the ties and pins out of her hair. "Are you feeling all right, Princess?"

"Yes, just tired."

"I thought you'd be up all night again."

"I was not up all night yesterday," Vonica said with a little laugh.

"Mm hmm," Mary said. "I wasn't sure I'd be able to wake you this morning early enough to do your hair."

"Then you can understand why I'm tired now."

"I also understand that you can sleep in the wheel house and that you won't see the other princesses for weeks or even months."

"I'm just tired."

"All right. Forgive me for intruding."

"I want to get an early start tomorrow."

"I'll let the kitchen and Sir Cyril Bright know."

"Thank-you Mary."

Mary hung Vonica's dress and said, "Shall I open the window?"

"Please. Some fresh air would be nice."

Mary finished puttering and paused at the door. "Princess, I hope you forgive me if I occasionally speak out of turn or overstep my role. I'm only a servant and I'm honoured to serve so closely. Please know I only speak out because I care."

"You've been doing it since you started, has it been five years already? If I haven't chased you off yet I don't think I will."

Mary smiled.

"Good-night, Mary."

"Good-night Princess."

19th of Daggerrise 24th Year of the 11th Rebirth
Stone's Shore, Stone Clan Province

Rheeya didn't try to stop the yawn but she was polite enough to hide it behind a hand. "Why are you leaving so early? You could stay another day or two you know. Betha and Taeya are."

"I know but my stewards are expecting me home."

"So write them. You're safe here."

"I really should return. I've left them to deal with the aftermath of the investigation."

"Ah, yes. I faced quite a few complaints after the whole mess with Evan and Jared Iron-Smith. And with Tomas needing time to heal, well, at least Master Hearth-Glow was a big help."

"Seems to run in the family."

"So you were telling me. Are you sure this Adorjan Hearth-Glow is not your prince? You had a lot to say about him."

"No, he is not. But I did assign him as the new steward to the Sun-Song estate, where the fire was. He is engaged to Lord Sun-Song's daughter now."

"Sounds like Dwayne Black-Mountain."

"I hope I have the good fortune of being able to attend Adorjan's wedding. Seems this parade of suitors they put us through is good for finding trustworthy friends at least."

"And weeding out untrustworthy ones as well. What's wrong? You seem suddenly down."

"Just thinking of how difficult my stewards will be when I return home," Vonica lied. Her thoughts had turned to Johann at the mention of the Sun-Song family. "With your soul bond complete you should be allowed to travel more. You must come and visit me."

"Perhaps soon. Master Hearth-Glow tells me I have much to do. The quickest way to see me would be to announce your wedding."

Vonica forced a smile. "I'm sure it won't be long now. Ah, here's Sir Cyril."

"Princess. Princess." His bow was sharp and precise. "Princess Vonica, we are ready whenever you are."

"Thank-you Cyril."

Rheeya threw her arms wide and embraced her friend. "Safe travels. May the sun guide your path. Write as soon as you get home."

Vonica received so few hugs now, with the other girls gone and her schedule too full to visit their old nanny anymore. It was so easy to forget how good a hug felt. As she closed her arms around her friend she thought, *I wonder if Johann – no.* She cut the thought short and stepped back. "I will write. May the sun ever shine upon you and yours."

Rheeya stayed out on the steps long after Vonica's party was gone through the gate. A servant came out to inform her that breakfast was ready.

"Yes," she said. "I'll be there. Is James already there?"

"Yes, Princess."

"Then I'll have to hurry or he'll eat all my toast."

24th of Daggerrise 24th Year of the 11th Rebirth
Sun Temple, Sun Temple Province

Vonica scanned the courtyard. Aside from the stable boys and servants milling around and the occasional noble out for a stroll the only others in the courtyard, and the only two who appeared to be waiting for her, were Salazar and Antony. She looked around again but there was no sign of Johann anywhere.

Why would he be waiting? He didn't know when you'd return.

"Princess, welcome home," Antony said. "You had a good trip I hope?"

"Yes. No troubles on the road. Sir Cyril will have a full report."

"And your fellow princesses?"

"All well, though Mallory seemed ... I don't know. Prince Kaelen did not seem at all happy though."

"He has ties to the Iron Guild," Antony said. "You girls have set the whole guild on its ear."

"Needed to be done," Vonica said with a coolness that surprised even her. "I'd like to go in and bathe. Is there anything I need to take care of this evening?"

"Not at all," Antony said. "Best if you just rest. We have much to do tomorrow."

Vonica frowned. She'd fully expected to be bombarded with complaints and tasks. Or at least she expected Antony to scold her for her tone. "Were there any letters for me?"

"Everything that came was left on your desk," Salazar said. "There wasn't much."

"Thank-you. I'll see you both in the morning."

After her bath and a quiet dinner alone Vonica turned her attention to the pile of letters. It was small, as Salazar promised. She flipped through, ignoring most of them on the seal alone. She kept the one from Adorjan aside then went through the pile again. It was no use. The letter she wanted to read was not there.

Pushing her disappointment aside she opened Adorjan's letter. It was an update, as she expected. His engagement was finalized and made official, as was his position as steward. She smiled. *I am happy for you, Adorjan.*

The only part of his letter that was puzzling was the mention of festivities on the twenty-seventh. If he was planning his wedding for that day he wasn't leaving her much time.

"Ah well," she said, setting the letter aside. "There's nothing to do for it now. I'll speak to my stewards in the morning."

25th of Daggerrise 24th Year of the 11th Rebirth
Sun Temple, Sun Temple Province

She took breakfast in the small dining room where she had dined with her suitors and was soon joined by her stewards. Salazar seemed nervous, not quite meeting her eye. Antony came in with a folder of papers.

"That's not my to-do list, is it?" she said, eyeing the papers.

"Of course not. It's not really a list at all. It's the first item on your to do list."

"First item? All that?"

He nodded.

She sighed. "Please eat, both of you, there's plenty. And it appears we'll be here a while." She had a short reprieve as her stewards settled in and served themselves. "I'm glad you didn't hand it to me last night. What is this about?"

"A formality, really, as the invitations were already sent. These are the replies."

"Invitations? Replies? Wait, does this have anything to do with whatever is happening on the twenty-seventh?"

Antony's smile faltered. "What do you know about the twenty-seventh?"

"Not much, except for the mention of festivities. And by the looks of those replies I'd guess you went ahead and planned a ball without permission or approval."

"After your resistance to being involved in any of the planning I didn't think you'd mind."

"How could you do this? I didn't want to plan a ball because I didn't want to host one at all!"

"I had little choice, My Lady."

"Little choice, not 'no choice'. You could have chosen to wait for me to return. I don't want this ball."

"I can't cancel it now."

"Then you put on the dress and go to the ball because I don't want to!"

Salazar covered his smile with a hand. Antony just gawked, his face growing redder by the second. "Princess Vonica!"

"Scold all you like. You'll look fetching."

"That's enough! You'll go. And you'll spend the next two days with me going over every detail. Except for your dress fitting appointments of course."

"Dress fittings? You scheduled me dress fittings?"

"Of course."

"Why?"

"To make you a new dress for the ball. And to begin work on your wedding dress."

"I don't need a new dress. I have dozens of dresses, and four wedding dresses!"

"Hmm, well, you could mention that to the seamstress. Perhaps there is something she could do to freshen one up for the occasion. Your first meeting with her is after breakfast. We have just enough time to review the replies to the invitations."

She glanced at Salazar, her eyes wide, pleading silently for his aid.

"I'm sorry Princess but I cannot stay and assist you with this. I have an important meeting that I cannot miss."

"Are you free for the midday meal?"

"Are you asking me to dine with you?"

"Yes, I am."

Salazar stood and bowed. "I will be there. Excuse me."

Vonica nodded and turned her attention to Antony and his pile of letters. "All right. Let me see these replies."

Vonica met Salazar back in the dining room at midday. "How was your meeting?" Vonica said.

"Productive. Yes, I think everything is on the proper course."

"Everything? Do you really think this ball is necessary?"

"Not as simple a question as it seems I'm afraid. Is it necessary for you? No, not at all. Is it necessary for Master White-Cloud? Absolutely. He needs to feel like he's doing something, contributing in some way to this important process."

"Is that why you didn't stop him?"

"My Lady, I'm not sure I could have stopped him if I had tried. And he went behind my back as well. He's been meeting with noble families for weeks, listening to their complaints, all so he can tell you he has to plan this ball to keep them happy. He may honestly believe it himself."

"So there is no way to stop this?"

"You are the Sun Temple Princess, we live to serve. If you command this to stop and Antony refuses you can remove him from his position as steward. It hasn't been done in generations and he may not take you seriously. Do not threaten if you don't mean to follow through."

Vonica paled. "I'm not sure I'm ready to go that far."

"Then there will be a royal ball in two days' time."

27th of Daggerrise 24th Year of the 11th Rebirth
Sun Temple, Sun Temple Province

Johann hurried out to the courtyard. Based on his sister's last letter he was probably running late but none of the servants rushing frantically past seemed to be looking for him so he couldn't be that late. For the last two days more and more noble families had been arriving in the Capital. Most stayed at estates or fancy boarding houses in the city, only a few with close family already living in the temple complex had the privilege of boarding there.

Johann burst out into the sunlight. The crystal clear sky would be interpreted as a sign of Airon's favour, Johann was sure of it. The courtyards were just as busy as the hallways but with the added confusion of horses and wagons and carriages.

One carriage in particular caught his attention as he weaved through the throng of people.

"Hail! Adorjan!"

Adorjan turned. "Johann! It's good to see you friend. Though I suppose we're to be brothers now." He shook Johann's hand.

"Soon enough," Johann agreed. "Where is my sister?"

"Here." She climbed down from the carriage. "And Mother too." She embraced him. "I wish you would have written after you left."

"I wasn't sure if would reach you."

"Master Ferrand would have found a way."

"I didn't want to put his job at any further risk." He turned. "Mother, it's good to see you again. I'm sorry about my sudden departure."

"Oh, don't worry. Your father can be a difficult man." She hugged her son and kissed his cheek.

"Where is Father? I didn't think anything would keep him away from the Capital today."

"Of course he's here. The last royal ball was held the year I was born. Your father was five. We wouldn't miss this for the world. He and your brother are talking to the stable master and the service staff so we can get settled. Your father is convinced our staying here and not in the city is a sign of Airon's favour on your brother. We haven't the heart to tell him it's because of Ioanna's engagement to Adorjan and Adorjan's ties to the princess."

"Speaking of which, Ioanna and I are meeting Vonica this morning, before her stewards force her into seclusion to prepare for the evening."

Johann sighed. "I'm envious."

Adorjan laid a sympathetic hand on Johann's arm.

"No, don't feel badly for me. I've had help while you were away."

"All right. We'll see you later then."

"And what exactly was that about?"

Johann turned back to his mother. "I'm just missing my academic partner. It's not as enjoyable, working alone."

"Life moves on," she said. "We were all surprised when Adorjan returned and we discovered he knew you. We hadn't realized that the two of you worked together."

He tried not to feel guilty about the deliberate misdirection. He took his mother's hand and tucked it in the crook of his arm. "Let me help you find your rooms."

"Come in," Vonica called. She stood at the window playing with the pendant around her neck.

"Is Antony White-Cloud still employed here?"

She turned and smiled. "Adorjan! You made it. I was starting to worry."

"Someone has to keep you sane. Vonica, may I introduce Ioanna Sun-Song who does me the honour of soon being my wife. Ioanna this is Vonica Bright-Rose, eleventh of her name, and if I start listing her titles she's liable to slap me."

"You're in a jovial mood I see." Vonica turned to the girl, so different from her brother it was hard to see the similarities. She was glad of that just now. She didn't want to think of Johann. "Welcome. I understand this is your first time in the Capital. You can call me Vonica when we're alone like this, I prefer it. In public people expect titles so it's better to use one or two."

"Thank-you. It's a great honour."

"Make sure Adorjan shows you more of this place than just the library. Unless of course you are like me, in which case you'll never want to leave the library. But come, sit, I'm guessing he dragged you over here the second you arrived, didn't he?"

"Yes," Ioanna laughed. "But to be fair he was concerned about you."

Vonica smiled. "There's no need for that. The last two days were overwhelming but today I feel balanced, at peace almost. But let me send for some food and then we can sit and talk until Master Antony sends for me. You have to tell me all about your village."

The sun was setting. Guests were coming down from their rooms or arriving in fancy carriages. Lady Sun-Song and her daughter were having their hair brushed and pinned. Ioanna's stomach was all aflutter. She didn't have to worry about admirers, of course. She was unknown at court and would be on the arm of her betrothed all night.

And you have permission to call the princess by her first name. How many others have that privilege?

In the adjacent room Lord Sun-Song and Tullius were picking at the remains of their dinner and waiting on the ladies of the family.

"This is your one chance to make a good impression," Yannakis said.

"I know, but how can I? No one knows anything about her."

"I told you to talk to Adorjan. Didn't he give you any information?"

"He said not to mention her scar, or stare at it."

"That was it?"

"He seemed reluctant to talk about her."

"Hmm. Do you think he regrets his choice? Or perhaps he is trying to hinder your chances while helping a member of his own family."

"Dear, I'm not sure it works that way," Francesca said, coming to the door. "Either Tullius is the prince or he isn't. No amount of coaching will change that. Are you two ready?"

Yannakis wiped his face. "Yes, we were just waiting for the two of you."

"Well then, we should go. Adorjan will be waiting in the main foyer."

In the scholar's wing Johann adjusted his tabard a third time. He brushed at an imagined dusty spot and looked at the small, cloudy mirror on his wall again. "You'd better get going," he told his reflection. "Salazar is waiting for you. This is it. I hope the priests are right about their good omens."

Vonica was still in a dressing gown. Mary was combing her hair while another girl fused with the dress and shoes. She was still, calm, almost detached. Her mind was strangely empty. She felt neither excitement nor dread.

She moved only when it was required and spoke only in answer to direct questions.

The dress belonged to a previous Vonica, the fifth rebirth if she was remembering correctly. The seamstress had adjusted the fit and added a contrasting trim around the collar and sleeves. The girls helped her into her dress and finished pinning her hair.

A casual glance at the mirror was enough to shake the calm that had gripped her since morning. All day the ball had felt like some distant thing. Now it felt immediate and inescapable.

Perhaps I should have them loosen the corset just a touch. Maybe that would make it easier to breathe? Why is it so warm in here all of a sudden?

There was a sharp knock at the door. "Are you decent?"

"Yes, come in Master Antony."

"Ah, you look lovely this evening. She did a marvelous job on your dress. The guests are arriving as we speak. Are you ready?"

"Of course." A few hours ago she'd felt confident, unshakeable. Now she could feel all that slipping away. She held out her hand and he helped her to her feet. "Let's go."

The palace wing was strangely quiet. Antony led her to the small receiving room adjacent to the ball room. "Wait here. Once all the important guests have arrived I'll signal the music and the doormen will open the doors. Do you remember what to do? What to say?"

She nodded. Already it was difficult to speak.

Antony returned the nod and disappeared out the side door.

She waited, her hands clasped against her skirt, her back straight. She started to twist her hands, tugging at her fingers and skirt. She chewed her lower lip and glanced about. The guards were paying no attention to her. She shifted her weight from one foot to the other and back again.

Her calm continued to slip away, her thoughts meandering away from solid and balanced and accepting. Doubt crept in, then concern, then fear, that familiar cold fist wrapping around her lungs until she couldn't breathe.

What are you doing? You couldn't handle meeting them one at a time. What makes you think you can do this? What will happen when they start asking questions that you don't want to answer? Antony will have a guard at every door. You can't run and hide this time. Maybe now yet. Maybe if you leave now. Tell the guard you're going to the …"

The music began with a sudden flourish that made her gasp. Her heart was suddenly beating too hard. She tried to take a deep breath but it came out shuddery. She stood a little straighter.

Calm down. Just calm …

The door opened. Stiff steps carried her through the doorway until she stood alone at the top of the great stairs. The musicians continued to play. The room was lit with candles and lanterns. Still the gathered faces seemed lost in shadow. And there were a lot of faces. And they were all looking at her.

That's right; they're all looking at you, at your scar. That's all they see. That's all anyone will ever see. The blessing of Airon? The strongest princess? How could anyone ever see that when you tremble in the face of a royal ball?

The music had stopped.

When did the music stop? What am I supposed to say?

She cleared her throat. "Welcome, everyone. I uh, thank you all for coming. Uh …" She glanced around, her gaze stopping on Antony. He was making a rolling motion with his arms, prompting her to continue. "I … uh … I hope everyone has a good time." *That sounded lame.* "I am sorry I had to delay all those meetings. I appreciate your patience."

Antony was frowning.

Why is he frowning? I'm saying the wrong thing. Something about duty? Honour? What was it?

"Uh, please ... no, I mean, I think we should begin now."

Antony closed his eyes, still frowning.

No, that was wrong. Oh, how could I forget?

Movement caught her attention and she looked down. The nobles had gathered right up to the foot of the stairs. Johann was three steps up, his hand on the railing. She'd been so caught up looking at the crowd she hadn't noticed him until now.

He wasn't wearing his usual robes; scholar's robes would have looked out of place here among the furs and silks and velvets and jewels.

The scholar's robes suit him.

He was halfway up the stairs now and people were starting to talk. Antony looked up. His eyes went wide. He took a step forward.

Salazar grabbed his arm. "Wait old friend, just wait."

Vonica's attention was on Johann alone as he made his way slowly up the stairs. "Hey," he said softly.

"What are you doing?" she whispered back.

"You look like you're panicking."

"They're staring."

He stepped right in front of her, blocking their view of her, and her view of them. "You're beautiful, of course they're staring."

"They're staring at the scar."

"I'm not."

She looked away.

"Vonica." He touched her cheek.

Her head snapped up, her eyes finding his. His hand was so warm. No one touched her, aside from the girls who dressed her and did her hair. She could only stare at him.

"You were so afraid because I'm an artist. An artist worships beauty, isn't that what you said? Don't you trust me?"

"Of course I do."

"I think you're beautiful, Vonica, and I'm an artist so I know what beauty is when I see it." He leaned down and kissed her.

Antony had broken free of Salazar and was halfway up the stairs when a light flared up around Johann and Vonica so bright he had to stop and cover his eyes.

Vonica smiled at Johann as the light faded. "I guess Airon is pleased."

"I don't care. I'm very happy."

"That seems like a blasphemous thing to say, especially now that you're a prince."

"He can smite me later."

Salazar had joined Antony on the steps and now he cleared his throat. Johann stepped over next to his blushing princess. Salazar smiled and then winked at Vonica before turning to address the crowd. "My Lords and Ladies may I introduce to you Princess Vonica Bright-Rose and Prince Johann Sun-Song. We are ecstatic to announce their engagement. How fortunate you are all here to celebrate with us. It pleases me greatly to be able to say that the pact is once again secure. Well, I know I'm not following any script. Someone start the music!"

Johann escorted Vonica down the stairs and for a long time they were busy greeting guests and accepting congratulations. Ioanna squeezed through the crowd an embraced Vonica. "This is so exciting. Now we have two weddings to plan. And now we'll be sisters. I always wanted a sister."

"I've missed having a sister so close," Vonica said.

Beside them Adorjan and Johann were shaking hands. "About time," Adorjan said.

"I never did ask, how long did you know?"

"The first time I saw the two of you together. When did you know?"

"That first day in the library."

They were joined by the rest of the Sun-Song family. Lady Sun-Song hugged her son then curtsied before Vonica as Johann introduced them.

"Vonica, this is my mother, Lady Francesca Sun-Song, my father, Lord Yannakis Sun-Song, and my elder brother, Tullius."

"An honour," Lord Sun-Song said.

"I guess the priests had the right idea but the wrong brother," Tullius said, clapping Johann on the shoulder. "Now I understand why you were in such a rush to return to the Capital."

"You could have told me," Yannakis said.

"I thought if I mentioned I was friends with Vonica you'd use that to gain an introduction for Tullius. You were fairly single-minded about this whole thing."

"I suppose I was. I'm sorry. You are both welcome at the Sun-Song estate any time."

"You'll stay until the wedding, won't you?" Vonica said.

"Of course," Francesca said. "We would be honoured. Oh, but of course we have Adorjan and Ioanna's wedding to plan."

"We're closer to my family if we stay here," Adorjan said.

"We could save a lot of time and just hold the weddings on the same day," Vonica said.

"Oh, I don't know about that," Adorjan said. "Your wedding involves some fairly unique blessings."

"We'll talk to the stewards first," Johann said.

"How many other engagements will be announced tonight and tomorrow I wonder?" Adorjan said.

"Too many," Johann replied. "I don't mean to brush you aside, you're family after all, but Vonica and I should mingle."

"Go on," Yannakis said, "We'll have time to talk tomorrow. For now I'll just drag Tullius around and see if I can't add his engagement to the list."

"Now hold on just a minute," Tullius said. "Engagement?"

28th of Daggerrise 24th Year of the 11th Rebirth
Sun Temple, Sun Temple Province

Johann joined Vonica for a late breakfast. "How did you sleep?" he said.

"I was exhausted," Vonica said. "I've never talked to so many people in one day before. What about you?"

"Better than I'm likely to sleep for a while now. I've been informed that tonight I will be sleeping in a special suite of rooms down the hall from yours and not in my little scholar's cell."

"You'd have to move after the wedding."

"But then I'd have you there with me."

Vonica blushed. "Did you really know that first time we talked?"

"No. It was the first time. I felt you watching me and I wanted to turn, to see who was making the hair on the back of my neck stand up like that. You ran away so fast I barely caught a glimpse of you but my heart was doing backflips. I didn't understand it at all. And then I saw you and I couldn't believe it. I felt complete. I felt at peace."

"You never said anything."

"I tried to, that day before the fire. You were late and you left."

"I remember that. We're lucky Antony never found us and put an end to our visits."

He cleared his throat. "About that. I may have gone to Master Sun-Wise and explained. He was protecting you, making sure you had that time to get to know me."

"Really?"

Johann nodded.

"I never guessed."

He reached out and took her hand. "And now Master Antony should be able to relax. You've found your prince."

"Yes. And I'm so very glad it's you."

1st of Hoofrise 24th Year of the 11th Rebirth
Sun Temple, Sun Temple Province

Holding the weddings on the same day was impossible so Adorjan Hearth-Glow and Ioanna Sun-Song were married on the last day of Daggerrise with their families, including Alessandro Hearth-Glow and Princess Vonica, in attendance. At dinner they were joined by the other princesses and two princes and afterwards they all turned in early.

Now as the noonday sun streamed in the temple skylight Vonica and Johann waited in an antechamber for their signal to enter.

"How can you sit there so calmly?" Vonica said as she paced.

"You're just upset that Mary told you not to sit and wrinkle your dress."

"I'm not standing to eat."

He laughed. "Now wouldn't that be a sight."

A young man in acolyte's robes rushed in. "They're ready to start."

Johann stood and offered his arm to Vonica. "Good. I'm tired of waiting. You're not going to forget what to say, are you?"

She laughed. "No, I don't think so."

So Princess Vonica and Prince Johann said the oaths and stood for the blessings while every noble in the province watched. And Vonica didn't mind at all. She no longer cared who stared at her.

About the Author

Casia Schreyer lives in rural Manitoba with her husband and two children. She loves to read and knit. Rose in the Ash is her fourth full length novel.

About the Cover Artist

Sara Gratton lives in Winnipeg, Manitoba with her husband and two children. She enjoys singing and is a member of the local Sweet Adelines. This is her second time teaming up with Casia as a cover artist.

Coming Soon

Separation: Underground Book 2

Ethan is on his way to Complex 50 while Shawna stays behind in Complex 48 waiting for the transfer student who will be living with her family now. Their special gifts bound these twins tightly together. Now they must learn to handle living apart no matter what – because they will never see each other again.

Rose Without Thorns: Rose Garden Book 3

There is unrest across the Isle of Light. While attending a meeting with the other princesses Princess Betha Rose of Roses receives word of an emergency in her province of Evergrowth, one that involves a member of the Animalkin. She and Princess Taeya Living Rose agree to travel to Evergrowth together to deal with the problem.

But Taeya's presence in Evergrowth causes an even bigger problem, one that may shatter the sacred pact that protects their island.

Also By Casia Schreyer

ROSE GARDEN SERIES

Rose in the Dark
Rose From the Ash
Rose Without Thorns (2018)
Rose Alone (2019)
Rose at the End (2020)

UNDERGROUND NOVELS

Complex 48
Separation (2017)
Reunion (2017)
The Quest (2018)
Choices (2018)
Training (2019)
Rebels (2019)
Turncoats (2020)

And watch for the Underground Graphic Novels, coming soon!

OTHER NOVELS

Nothing Everything Nothing
Pieces

NON-FICTION

Mature and Responsible Adult – Sometimes (Digital only)

SHORT STORIES, POETRY, & INSPIRATIONAL

Easter Mysteries (Digital only)
ReImagined

NELLY-BEAN …
And the Kid Eating Garbage Can Monster (Available in English, French)
And the Adventures of Nibbles
And the Lost Bear (2018)
And the Messy Dragon (2019)

Made in the USA
Middletown, DE
29 May 2017